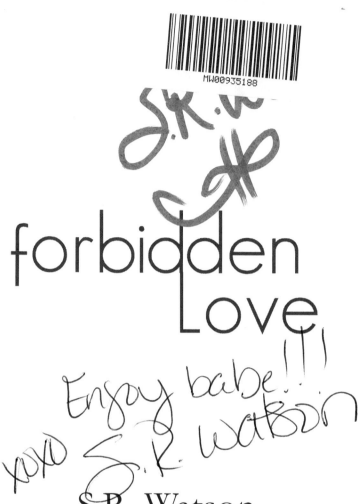

forbidden
Love

S.R. Watson

xoxo Enjoy babe!!! S.R. Watson

Cover Design: Sarah Hansen of Okay Creations
Editor: Vanessa Bridges of PREMA Romance
Formatter: Stacey Blake of Champagne Formats

ISBN-13: 978-1503162600
ISBN-10: 1503162605

dedication

To my mother, Clara Brown, who started it all.
She put the first book in my hand and inspired my
love for reading. This love evolved into a desire
to write and share my own stories.

My mother taught me about the power of
inspiration and courage, and she did it with
a strength and a passion that I wish could be
bottled.

~ Carly Fiorina

prologue

I LAY HERE literally and metaphorically broken, listening to my mom give Liam shit in the living room. He is here to visit again like he does every day. My mom tells him to limit his visit to an hour because I need my rest. *Yeah right.* That's all I've been doing is fucking resting. Jordan is away on some family retreat over winter break so my visitors are limited. I had plenty of family and old friends come by when I first came home, but people have since returned to the normalcy of their own lives. Without Liam, I would be going stir crazy. My mom still hasn't forgiven him for cheating and breaking my heart, but we're trying to work on our friendship. Neither Liam nor my mom, know about Grayson or our failed relationship; if you can call it that. I was his fuck buddy that he grew bored with. They don't know about my stalker either. They would go ape shit and go into overprotective mode. I did call Officer Richards last week to tell him the truth about the phone calls. They're looking into it. I haven't had any anonymous calls since I got home so for now, I'm trying not to think about it. Liam comes in carrying pupusas in a Styrofoam container. He introduced me to this Salvadoran goodness earlier this week. They are tortillas filled with cheese, pork, and refried beans. I love them.

"Hurry and give them to me," I demand jokingly. I reach for them, but he moves the container out of my reach before I can grab it.

"Nope. What do you say?" He taunts.

"Please. Now give them to me before I hurt you." I give him a megawatt smile that is supposed to convey that I'm plotting my vengeance.

"You couldn't leave it at please," he jokes. "Hurt me? I'm so scared. You can barely get out of bed. Besides who do you think will bring you more of these hot commodities if you hurt me?" He has a point.

"Fine." I love our banter. It serves as a solace from the heartache I feel when I'm alone with my thoughts and memories. He hands me the container and sits on the corner of my bed.

"How are you feeling today?" he asks, turning our conversation serious. I try to portray the picture of happiness, but every now and then I back pedal into depression and it shows. Everyone thinks it's because of my accident and having limited mobility. I don't tell them any differently.

"A little better. I've reduced my intake of pain meds so that's something." He cocks his head to the side and eyes me suspiciously—probably sensing there's more that I'm not sharing, but he is unsure what.

"Okay. Well, that's good," he replies not totally convinced. He gets up and grab a few board games from my closet. "So which game shall we play today?" My choices are Scrabble, Monopoly, and Checkers. I choose Checkers because I know that it is secretly his favorite. His face lights up at my choice and I can't help but laugh. Needless to say, he goes over the hour time limit my mother has for him. When she comes in to run him off, my eyes plead with hers to let him be. We play several games before I finally give up on the idea of trying to catch up to his number of wins. He puts everything away when my mom brings dinner in. He waves his good-bye and tells me he will see me the same time tomorrow. I don't miss the not-so-subtle eye roll that my mom gives him, but he does.

"That boy is still in love with you," she warns when he leaves.

"We're just friends Mom." I let out a deep breath. She doesn't realize just how appreciative I am of that friendship right now. "That chapter of our lives is over, but there is no reason we can't be great friends," I reason.

"Just be careful," she says before leaving me alone with my dinner. I devour the chicken breast and brussel sprouts. After the meal I had earlier, this is flavorless in comparison, but I know I need to balance my meals with the healthy stuff. Especially since, I'm not getting much activity. My ass really will have its own zip code. After my meal, I get ready for bed. I'm alone with my misery again and it sucks. Another day down and will reset tomorrow. It's a slow recovery, but I'm making strides. I turn out the lights and get into bed. This cast is a pain in the ass to sleep in, but I manage.

chapter
1

AS THE WHEELS of the plane touch down on the tarmac, the pilot announces our arrival to Los Angles. The butterflies in my stomach that have been lying dormant over the winter break flutters at the realization that I'm back in the same city as the man who possesses my soul. Until now, numbness occupied the place where my heart resides. I was in shock at the way things transpired back when I was lying there in the hospital bed. Grayson let Vanessa deter him from checking to see how I was doing after my accident. His termination of our arrangement hurt me, but his refusal to see me in the end was annihilation to my already fragile existence. I don't know what to do with these feelings that have resurfaced. Okay in fairness they never left, just suppressed.

My hands clutch the arm rests of my seat as I brace myself for the sudden halt of the plane to a complete stop. I hate flying. Jordan looks over and pats my hand in understanding. She knows just how much I detest flying and small spaces. Combine the two elements together and I am a total nut case. The window seat did very little to offset my anxiety. We only flew because we left Jordan's car back at the condo after my accident. I was too busted up to sit through a twenty-two hour drive home. Once the seat belt sign turns off, Jordan gets up quickly to grab our backpacks from the overhead storage. She then backs up to let me out, forcing the people behind her to wait until I ease into the isle in this God-awful boot.

It's a black medical boot with velcro straps that go with everything— not. It's a pain-in-my-ass contraption that makes my foot sweat, but it's a necessary evil for my healing ankle fracture. My orthopedic doctor anticipates that I will need to wear this fashionable piece of foot accessory for another three weeks. Well at least I was able to say adiós to the cast and crutches. It feels great to be able to get around independently now. My mom babied me the entire time I was home. Believe it or not, Liam was my only saving grace from the looney bin. Jordan's family whisked her off for most of the break for some sort of family retreat, but Liam visited me religiously. He would lose his shit if he knew about my stalker and the possible real cause of my accident. I did get in touch with the police officer though, to let him know the truth. He said he would look into it, but didn't have much to go on since my lie caused the investigation to be ruled an accident.

My mother placated me by letting Liam come over, but her own failed marriage has left her bitter. I reassured her that there was nothing left between us, but friendship. This eased her concerns some, but she continued to eye him with disdain. Liam was ignorant to her disapproval of his presence. His mother, on the other hand, was happy that we were working on our friendship. I suspect that she is holding on to the idea that our friendship will blossom into what we had. *That ship has more than sailed.*

After we obtain the rest of our luggage and walk towards the front entrance of the airport, Jordan informs me that Bailey is picking us up. I pause in fear of what's on the other side of those automatic doors.

"Shiv, I promise it's just Bailey. I made her promise to come alone. She thought the request was odd, but she told me the others won't be back until Sunday."

"It's not the girls I'm worried about." I gnaw at my bottom lip.

"No Vanessa either. And of course Grayson would have no reason to be riding with her."

When we walk out, Bailey is standing next to her Range Rover. She spots us immediately and runs up to give me a hug.

"Oh my god. I've missed you guys so much." She gives me a soft squeeze before looking me in the eye. "How are you feeling?"

"Good. I'm glad to be back. I can't wait to knock this semester out so we can finally graduate." Yeah, I lay the lie on thick. Truth is, I'm nervous about the potential of running into Grayson. I am taking another marketing class this semester with a different professor, but the possibility of a run in is still there since it will be in the same building. I strategically chose the days opposite of his teaching schedule just to lessen the odds. "I agree with that. I can't wait to graduate and start the next chapter of my life," Bailey says dreamily. "You know, meet my future husband, have two point five kids, and buy the house with the white picket fence."

She had me going for a second until I realize she is full of shit. She lives in a high-rise loft for God's sake. I shove her and laugh at her sarcasm. She turns and hugs Jordan in equal measure. She then lifts her trunk so that we can load our luggage, only she slaps my hand away when I try to lift my mine. These people and their babying are going to drive me crazy. Yes, my ribs still give me trouble at times and I'm in this damn boot, but I am not incapable of doing things for myself. This is my mother's behavior all over again. I don't make a scene, though. I know she's just trying to be helpful. I will just have to make sure the girls don't go overboard. I hate feeling helpless.

I slide into the back seat and put my Beats earbuds in my ears. Jarell Perry's "Win" croons through the earbuds and my mind once again falls on Grayson. I can already tell it's going to be harder to push him to the back of my thoughts now that I'm back in Los Angeles. Jordan taps my leg in an effort to get my attention. I pull one bud out so that I can hear what she is saying.

"We were going to stop for a bite to eat before going home and I wanted to see if you had a place in mind."

"It doesn't really matter. Whatever you two decide, I'll be good with."

Now that she mentions it, I am kind of hungry. The snack on the plane did very little to curb my appetite.

"Well, I did have a craving for Chinese food," Jordan offers.

"Craving, huh? You have something you're not telling me?" Bailey catches on immediately and hysterically slaps the steering wheel. Realization crosses Jordan's face and she pinches my knee. "Ow, I can't believe you pinched me," I joke.

"I am not pregnant you goof ball. That would be an im-maculate conception seeing as though I haven't seen Trevor since before the break. That and I'm a firm believer in the saying—no glove, no love," she chuckles.

I don't let on that Grayson and I've had unprotected sex when we were exclusive. "Chinese sounds good. I love their hot and sour soup."

"Chinese it is then," Bailey confirms.

"Only you Shiv. No one else goes to a Chinese restaurant for the soup," Jordan teases.

WE FILL UP on General TSO's chicken and soup until we are completely stuffed. If I don't watch it, my stomach is going to be as big as my ass. When we get home, Bailey decides she is going to come up to our condo and hang out for a while. I excuse myself for some relaxation time in the tub. Back at my mother's house, I had to take showers because of the cast. My orthopedic doctor was thoughtful enough to transition me to a boot when he found out I was coming back to school for the spring semester.

As the tub fill with water, I pour in some of my hand-made lavender-infused jojoba oil. The flowery scent wafts in the air and relaxes me before I even get into the steaming hot bath. I rid myself of my clothes and save my boot for last. It feels good to let my foot breathe. I'm careful not to bear any weight on my right leg as I ease into the silky water. I lean back in the tub and I can't stop my thoughts from drifting to Grayson. This scene that I have set up for myself is similar to my last romantic night with him followed by awesome sex. My hand slips beneath the surface the water on its own accord. I gently stroke my clit as his face appears behind my closed eyes. I image his strong arms and wash-board abs and my legs begin to tremble as I stroke faster. In my fantasy, it is Grayson who is bringing me to the brink of an orgasm. I hear his voice whisper 'that's it baby,' and I explode in ecstasy. I bite my bottom lip to muffle my whimpers. Shameful, I know. I am supposed to be moving on from him. I blame it on being back here and all the damn memories we created.

Now that my skin is pruny like and I've rubbed one out, I get out of the tub and dry off completely before strapping my boot back on. I reluctantly put on a pair of sleep shorts and tank top, wishing I could just sleep naked and save myself the trouble putting on clothes. Jordan would get a kick out of that idea since she is the minimalist, clothing wise.

I'm not in bed long before Jordan is entering my room with two glasses of white wine. She sits on the edge of my bed and hands me one. "Did Bailey leave?"

"Yeah. She's having a get-together Sunday once Angie and Meghan get into town."

I give her my don't-even-ask look and she laughs. "Don't worry. I already lied and told her you had plans with Liam."

"That may not be a bad idea. I can call him tomorrow to see if he wants to do something."

"You're playing with fire, Shiv. He knows you well and is using time to work his way back into your heart," she huffs. "I have my eyes on him."

"You and my mother are insane. By the same logic, I know him too. He will not be sneaking past my defenses. We. Are. Just. Friends," I emphasize as I gulp the last of my wine.

"Okay. Whatever. Anyway, I have plans for us tomorrow morning so get some sleep." She takes my empty wine glass from me and literally skips out of the room. I know she is up to something, but right now I am too tired to care. I see that it is just shortly after one in the morning. I set the alarm on my phone for 8:00 a.m. before using the remote to turn out the light. Right now, this little invention is the best thing ever since sliced bread. I turn on my side, snuggle under the covers, and let sleep take me under.

THE EARLY MORNING light filters through my curtains and I feel the weight of Jordan's body holding my covers taunt against me. "Get up Shiv and get dressed. You're burning daylight."

My alarm has yet to go off so that tells me that it's not even eight yet. Jordan yanks the covers the rest of the way down as an incentive for me to get up. I feel like giving her a hard time so I groan my displeasure and pull the covers back over my head.

"Ah come on Shiv, don't be like that. Get up already. We're on a schedule."

I try to hold back my snickering, but it is useless. She pulls the covers back once again in this tug o' war we have going on and shows me her pout.

"Okay. Okay. Go on and get out already so I can get dressed."

"I don't know what you've got to hide. You know I've already seen your luscious goods. Just be glad that I'm straight, darling," she kids as she gets up to leave my room.

"I'm giving you twenty minutes and then I'm coming back," she warns.

I know that she is not bluffing either. I pull my phone from under the pillow and grimace at the time. It's six freaking forty-five. I really do groan this time. Jordan has lost her mind. What the hell is it possibly to do at this time of morning? This had better be good. I throw on a maxi dress and pair it with a blue jean jacket and ballet flats.

I told you the boot went with everything, as long as you don't attempt to wear jeans, leggings or anything else fitting. Right now it is nicely obscured underneath my dress. Of course Jordan looks like she just stepped off the pages of Vogue in her skinny jeans, off the shoulder sweater, heels, and the accessories to match. I'm neither surprised nor jealous. I'm not trying to keep up with my fashionista best friend. We are out the door by eight o'clock. The alarm on my phone goes off and I roll my eyes at the irony. Jordan just smiles because she knows that I would just be getting up right now.

"Are you going to tell me where we're going now?" I ask stifling a yawn.

"Nope. It'll ruin the surprise." *God I hate surprises.* She cranks up the radio when she hears Lana Del Rey's *Burning Desire* come on. I'm not a fool. She's trying to suppress any more questioning about where we're going. I fold my arms and look out the window. She continues her antics by singing loudly and off key. She tugs on my jacket and ask me to join in on the chorus and I do because I can't stay frustrated with her when she is being dorky. We pull up to The Landing luxury hotel and a valet attendant is at my door immediately escorting me out. Jordan comes around to join me.

I look at the elegance of the hotel and then back at her

in disapproval. She is obviously dressed for the likes of this place, where as I look like I missed my turn for the local Motel 6. "What the hell Jordan? A little warning would've been nice. I'm not dressed for this place," I admonish.

"Nonsense. There's no dress code for what I have planned. You'll see." She grabs me by the hand so that I will follow her. When the hotel's spa comes into view, I snatch my hand away. There's no way I can afford this and she is smoking crack if she thinks I'm letting her pay. I turn to leave, but she grabs me once again. "See this is why I wanted our spa day to be a surprise. I knew you'd react this way," she whines.

"Sorry, surprise or not, you've wasted your time." I feel a fight coming on and I hate fighting with her. She knows my stance on her spending money on me. I nearly choked on her utterance of spa day. Not a spa treatment as in singular, but a spa day as in getting a bunch of shit done and spending a lot of money.

"Just hear me out," she pleas. My dad just became a silent partner with this hotel chain. One of the perks is that his family and specified guest gets to enjoy the amenities at no cost. He told me to share this with some of my friends once I got back to Los Angeles. I only wanted to share it with my best friend. I want this to be our thing. Whenever we want." She looks genuinely sad. I love her to pieces. I can't deny her after she puts it that way. I hug her to convey my acceptance of such a wonderful gift. She squeals in delight and we are escorted to the locker room where we undress and put on robes.

We are given fruit-infused water while we wait for our personal masseuses to come get us for our massages. We spend the day indulging in caviar facials and massages, as well as manicures, pedicures, and hair treatments. We had a break in between for a healthy lunch, but now I am starving. Healthy stuff never sticks to you. I need something fattening ASAP. We make dinner plans to eat at the hotel's steakhouse. I'm too hungry to care about the other appropriately dressed patrons. I would die of starvation if I had to wait until we got home and then for Jordan to cook something. *Who knew all day pampering worked up an appetite.* The masseuse did say something about releasing toxins and yada... yada...yada. My body must've expended its entire energy source releasing said toxins.

Jordan and I enjoy a nice steak dinner and several glasses of wine. Well, I do anyway. All is right in the world again. My stomach has reached capacity and I have a nice buzz. Jordan only had one glass, stating she needs to be able to drive. She tells me to enjoy and I oblige.

"I'm glad we had this time to catch up, Shiv. I know our time together was cut short over this Christmas break since I ended up vacationing with my parents." She grabs my hand across the table and squeezes.

"No. I totally understood. I can admit, this was actually fun. Thank you."

"This will be our thing when we feel the need for a little pampering. Now let me order a bottle of wine like the one you've been guzzling and we can go," she smiles. I can't help but laugh. She orders a bottle of wine to enjoy once we get home and we leave. Once we get home, I take my clothes off and leave them in a pile next to my bed. As soon as my head hits my pillow, I am off to dreamland.

chapter
2

I GET UP around 11:00 a.m., enjoying the fact I was able to sleep in. Jordan has already left to go meet the girls at Bailey's place. I decide today is going to be a lazy day. Tomorrow we start classes so this is my last chance to enjoy having nothing to do. I contemplate calling Liam to hangout, but decide against it. This may be his last free day too. He should spend it how he chooses, not cooped up with someone he has absolutely no chance with. I make my way to the kitchen and start the Keurig to brew me a cup of coffee. On the counter, I find an omelet that Jordan has left for me in a Tupperware container. I smile at her thoughtfulness as I heat it in the microwave. This is so much better than the grill cheese sandwich I was prepared to make.

I take my brunch and sit in front of the television. Nothing good is on so I watch a recording of *American Idol*. I should totally audition for this show. I love music. That counts right? Okay, maybe not. After three hours in the same spot vegetating, I decide to make some soap. I have a new recipe I want to try with some New Zealand honey. I think I'll call it Manuka Honey and Oats. I head to the kitchen to gather my supplies. After my preparation, I set about mixing everything. I add honey, vanilla essential oil, oatmeal for exfoliation, and coconut milk to my formula. The final result smells heavenly.

Jordan may just have a new favorite. I pour the mixture into a wooden mold and wrap it with a quilt before putting it in a dark place to saponify, also known as the back of my closet. Jordan picks this time to check on me. My phone plays her Lana Del Rey ringtone *This is What Makes Us Girls*.

"Hey Jor," I yawn.

"Oh my God. Tell me you are not just getting up?"

"Shut up. I've been up since eleven smart ass."

"Yeah, because that's early. I knew you were going to sleep in. What have you done all day?"

"I have, you know I made soap today. Just finished actually," I defend.

"Yay! What kind did you make? Do I get a loaf?"

I knew that would get her attention. "Calm down crazy person. You don't get a loaf this time because I only made one. You still haven't used all of your other loaf I gave you."

"Whatever. I can still want more. So don't keep me in suspense. What kind did you make?" I can tell she is becoming impatient.

"This scent is new. It's called Manuka Honey and Oats." I continue to tell her the ingredients of the soap.

"Ooh. I can't wait to try it." Soap is supposed to cure for at least four to six weeks, but we always steal a bar after the saponification process is done, which is usually the next day. "Okay, you side tracked me with the mention of the

15

soap. I called to tell you I wouldn't be home for dinner. The girls and I are going to hang out a little longer. I won't be out too late since we start class in the morning."

"No worries Jor. I can cook dinner for myself." And it's true. I can manage things that come in a box. I hear snickering on the other end of the line.

"Just don't burn the place down," she teases.

"Hush. I can cook when I want to. Too bad you're going to miss out on this gourmet meal I'm planning." That does it. She is laughing hysterically now. I hang up on her. I can cook. I put a pot of water on the stove to boil and pour myself some white wine. I've gone from hardly drinking to being a lush in one semester. I open a pouch of albacore tuna and set it aside. I look through the pantry and score a box of Kraft macaroni and cheese. I also see a can of Rotel tomatoes. Who says I can't cook? After the macaroni and cheese cooks, I add in the tuna, tomatoes, and top it off with Cajun seasoning. It is so good. I think I'll return Jordan's earlier sentiment. I put some aside for her in a Tupperware container.

I polish off two more glasses of wine while I lay my clothes out for the morning. It's close to midnight now and we both have a long day ahead of us tomorrow. Our first class starts at eight. We planned our long day of classes to be the same so we could carpool. She doesn't need much sleep like I do, so she'll be fine. I set my alarm on my phone and snuggle under my covers. I'm proud that I was able to keep my thoughts of Grayson to a minimum today.

"Shiv, get up," Jordan sings as she bounces on my bed. How in the hell does she always manage to get up so early?

"What time is it?" I groan at the fuzziness in my head. Maybe I went a little overboard with the wine. "And what time did you get in this morning?"

"It's a little after seven and I got in at one. Now get up or you're going to make us both late." She takes the covers completely off my bed and put them on the ottoman in the corner. "Be ready to go in twenty minutes lazy bones."

I get ready and meet her in the kitchen with two minutes to spare. The aroma of coffee wafts in the air. "I made the dark espresso roast. You look like you could use a boost."

"Thanks. We all can't be morning people." I roll my eyes at her perceptiveness. I get the biggest travel mug I can find and add a second cup of coffee to it.

The ride to school brings on my anxiety about running into Grayson. I don't have my marketing class until tomorrow, but I am nervous about seeing him around campus. I try to think logically about how big the campus is and the odds are in my favor. Jordan I make plans to meet for breakfast after our first class and then I'm left alone with my fear as I head off to class.

THREE CLASSES LATER, Jordan and I meet up by the library as planned before heading home. She mentions the girls are meeting at our place to start margarita Mondays again.

"Didn't you guys just see each other yesterday?" I grouse. I plan on getting in the bed much earlier tonight and I don't want to even see any alcohol.

"Yes, but we want to continue our tradition. This is our last semester before everyone goes in different directions," she pleas. "And absolutely no Vanessa."

"You can't be sure. You know Bailey likes to invite her

along to these things," I huff.

"No, I can promise," Jordan insists. "I saw her at Bailey's get-together yesterday and I told her that I would beat her skinny ass if she set foot here again."

I can't help but smile. Jordan is the nicest person you ever meet until you get on her bad side, then you better watch out. "No you didn't," I chortle. "What did she say?"

"She didn't say anything. She's no fool. She turned her bony ass around and left the room. She was only there because she knew Grayson was there."

The smile disappears from my face in a nanosecond. "What? Grayson was there? You weren't—," She cuts my inquisition off.

"Sorry, that was a slip. We're not talking about him remember? You're supposed to be moving on. Besides there's nothing to tell. He just stopped by to pick something up from Bailey. He had one drink and then he left."

"Did he ask about me?" I can't help but wonder if I am constantly on his mind too.

"Damn Shiv. No he didn't. It was better that he didn't. I don't know if I could have contained the can of whip ass that was dying to come out the minute he walked through the door." She's getting worked up just on the recollection alone. I know this conversation is done. "Now we are going to have the girls over, drink our asses off, and you will not give one thought to that jackass."

I stay quiet because I'm not interested in partying. When we get home, I head straight to my room and change into sweats before returning to the kitchen and plopping my books on the counter. I look through the syllabus of my classes as Jordan prepares dinner. She said she ate the meal I left for her when she came in this morning and that it was actually pretty good. However, I'm glad she is back to take over the cooking duties. I clean and she cooks. It's a match made in heaven. Lord help me if I ever find a husband. My mind lands on Grayson again and I pinch my nose in frustration.

"You have a headache?" Jordan asks.

"No just tired," I lie. Well not totally, I guess. "I think I'm going to eat and just show my face for a little bit before I turn it for the night."

"Fair enough," she agrees. Tomorrow we only have one class as it is our short day. For me though, I have my marketing class in that building. His teaching day was today, but I am still anxious over the possibility of a run in.

MY PHONE ALARM shrills in the distance and I nearly fall out of the bed trying to determine the source of the noise. As I wipe the sleep from my eyes, I become more oriented and realize that it is time for me to get up. I fumble around my pillows and sheets until I find my phone and turn off the alarm. I'm actually able to get ready before Jordan comes to get me up. That is an accomplishment in itself. I pull my waist length red tresses in a messy bun. I didn't have the patience to dry it completely so, bun it is. When I walk into the kitchen, Jordan is sitting at the counter dressed and talking on her phone. I'm guessing from her now hush tones that she is talking to Trevor. I grab my travel mug already filled with coffee and a banana. Jordan gets up and heads to the door, never ending her call so I take that as my cue that is time to go.

AS I WALK into the building that houses my marketing class, I wipe my sweaty hands on my jeans. This building brings back so many memories. When I walk through doors, I am incapable of keeping my eyes from shifting to the second floor where Grayson taught. My heart rate speeds up and it isn't until I cross the threshold of my class here on the first floor that I realize that I had been holding my breath.

I look around the auditorium styled seating and quickly find a seat in the middle row. I hate being the center of attention so I quickly make my way there. We're all waiting for the professor to arrive. It is now five minutes after the hour and students are beginning to leave — claiming the five-minute rule. The other half of the class, including myself, don't want to chance it. Another ten minutes go by and you can tell the remaining students are starting to get a bit antsy. They're checking their watches and watching the door with apt attention.

I have just begun to put my things back in my messenger bag when the voice that has been intruding my thoughts comes from the front of the class.

"Good morning, everyone. I'm Professor Michaels. Professor Grant had a family emergency this morning and could not be here." *No. No. No. This can't be happening.* This is my worst nightmare realized. "You chose to stay and it will not go unnoticed. I am going to take attendance so that those of you who stayed can get credit. After that, I will share with you a few additions to add to your syllabus before letting you all leave."

My heart is racing again. He's standing in front of the class looking like a wet dream in his denim jeans and button down shirt. His inky black hair has grown out some and looks even more like just-fucked locks.

"Amy Gaines," he calls. Oh God, he is getting closer to my name. And then it happens. "Siobhan Gallagher," he says stumbling over his words.

His eyes begin to scan the classroom in his search for me. I timidly raise my hand. "Here," I murmur. Our eyes meet briefly, but I can't hold his gaze. My initial lust for him is replaced with anger as I recall all the memories that left me a heart broken mess. He finishes calling attendance and proceeds to give us the additions to the syllabus. After his dismissal, the students rush out like the building is on fire. This stupid boot impedes my quick escape and now he is waiting for me to make my way down the aisle. His face pinches in sympathy when he sees my boot, but he doesn't mention it.

"Siobhan," he begins uncertainly. He looks around to ensure that every student has left. "How are you feeling?"

"Oh now you want to pretend to care?" I sneer.

"I do care. Can we talk?" He grabs me by the shoulder to keep me from walking out of the class. His eyebrows knit together in a scowl. A flash of something crosses his beautiful features, but he slips his unreadable mask back up too quickly for me to decipher what.

"Let go of me. We have nothing left to discuss. You laid it all out for me that day back at the apartment and then you proceeded to drive the message home at Bailey's condo." He hesitantly removes his hand from my shoulder. He is about to say something else, but then his forehead crinkles in disgust. I follow his eyes and see that Liam is walking towards us. I decide to turn it up a notch.

"Hey babe. What are you doing here?" Other than the slight eyebrow rise at the endearment, Liam doesn't miss a beat.

"I knew you only had one class today and that you should be out soon. I missed hanging out with you Sunday so I thought you may want to grab breakfast this morning." You could bounce a quarter off of Grayson's face it was so hard. The slight twitch of his jaw lets me know he is beyond pissed. *Good.*

"Sounds like a plan, let's go. I'll text Jordan and tell her where to meet us when she gets out." I turn to Grayson and turn the knife I've already inserted. "Nice seeing you again Professor Michaels. Take care." I see a flash of something that looks like hurt, but it can't be. He dumped me.

Liam takes my messenger bag like a doting boyfriend would and we head toward the cafeteria. Liam immediately heads to the grill while I make my way to the waffle-making station. I sent Jordan a text on our way here so I thought it was her texting me when my phone chirps. *Wrong.*

Grayson: Are you FUCKING him? You took that cheating bastard back?

Wow, he is even more pissed off than I originally thought.

Me: That is no longer your concern. VANESSA IS!!!

I silence my phone. He has no reason to be upset. He didn't want me. When I make it to the table that Liam found, I put on my mask of indifference and take a seat.

"So. What was with the baby comment?" Liam is smiling from ear to ear.

I knew that this was coming. *Crap.* "Sorry Liam. Bad joke, I know. I was only teasing, but then I realize it wasn't a good idea," I lie. He doesn't look like he's buying it. I would say by the shit-eating grin he's still wearing, he thinks it was a slip up. *Whatever.*

"No worries, *baby*." He emphasizes the word baby. "I know that we're just friends." He winks at me and I think we just took a couple of steps backwards. Jordan shows up out of nowhere and I couldn't be more grateful. She has food in hand so apparently she has been here for a minute. We finish our breakfast and Liam informs us that he is heading to his next class. Jordan and I are done for the day so we head home. I don't dare bring up Grayson again after the melt down she had the other day. She tells me that Bailey was going to be coming over in an hour so they could develop some type of study plan.

I purchase the new textbook that Grayson stated we would need and download it to my iPad. I prefer digital books for a lighter load and to just carry my laptop around with me. After looking at the syllabus for all four of my classes and developing my own study plan, I decide to take a nap. When I wake up it's evening time. I didn't mean to sleep that long.

chapter
3

I WALK TO the kitchen to make a sandwich since I missed lunch. Jordan's door is halfway open so I can see that she is on the phone. She is probably talking to Trevor again. I walk back to my room and set my phone on its iHome docking station. I'm in the mood for music. Stateless' "Bloodstream" fills the room and my mind falls on Grayson. The doorbell rings followed by heavy knocking. I can hear Jordan padding to the door so I resume my trance. Then I hear an angry Jordan and I go on alert.

"You can't be here you bastard. I'm calling the fucking police." Oh she is spitting mad. Her steps are louder now as two sets of footsteps head toward my door.

"Do what you must, sweetheart, but I'm not leaving without talking to her." *Damn.*

The door swings open and there he is. His eyes are pleading for me to hear him out. "You didn't answer my texts or my calls. We need to talk."

"She doesn't have shit to say to you, asswipe," Jordan

spits.

"Jordan, it's okay. I'll handle this. Let us have a minute." She rolls her eyes in frustration and stomps away. I know leaving was hard for her to do, but she is giving me the privacy I asked for. I cross my arms over my chest and Grayson's eyes immediately keen in on my now lifted breasts. It is only now that I realize that I'm only in a camisole and panties.

I shrug my shoulders. Well, it's not like he hasn't seen me naked. "What do you want, Grayson?"

"Are you back with Liam? Are you fucking him?" His hands are balled into fists at his side.

"That's none of your business. Next question." He actually growls at my response before taking a deep breath.

"Okay. Let me try again. I want to start by apologizing that I didn't come see you in the hospital. I feel like it was all my fault."

"So you're here out of guilt? Let me save you the trouble. It's not your fault. It was the rain." I don't tell him that I was crying my eyes out. "And you did come. You just let Vanessa talk you out of seeing me. There was no need to tarnish your reputation for me."

He closes the distance between us. He reaches for me, but then lets his hands fall to his side when he sees my opposing stance. "Oh baby, is that what you thought? You couldn't be further from the truth." He has the nerves to reach for me again, but I back away. Meanwhile "Bloodstream" continues to play like a soundtrack for our reunion.

"Oh no. You don't get to call me that. You left me remember?" He flinches at my accusation.

"I'm sorry that you had to hear that, but if you were listening, you'd know that I had to leave." He starts pacing back and forth. "I left to protect you. Not me. I—,"

"Bullshit. I didn't ask you to protect me." He rushes back over to me and pulls me into his arms, but I struggle to get free.

"I promise you, I didn't want to leave. I just couldn't risk your academic future by calling Vanessa's bluff."

I finally break free and we just stare at each other. Then the strangest thing happens. Grayson drops to his knees in surrender. His hands grasp my hips as he rests his head on my stomach. I can feel his labored breaths. The grip he has on my hips tightens to the point his arms are trembling. I'm frozen to this spot. He is barely holding it together and I'm caught off guard. I've never seen this side of him. He seems so broken. He keeps his head buried in my stomach as he begins to talk. "Tell me how to make this right, baby. I need to make us right again," he pleads.

"You dumped me, Grayson. And then you fucked Vanessa and rubbed my face in it at Bailey's house-warming." I try to separate myself from him, but he is still holding on tight.

"I got scared and pushed you away. I was scared because I fell in love with you. I am irrevocably in love with you."

"So let me get this straight. You fall in love with me, so you go and stick your dick in someone else? That's real comforting."

"I panicked, but I swear it would never happen again. I just wasn't ready. The last time I let love in, it nearly destroyed me." He looks up at me and a lone tear slides down his cheek. I know immediately that I have just lost my will to stay angry with him. Technically we were just fuck buddies so I didn't have a claim to him. And he did end it with me before sleeping with Vanessa. This rationalization still doesn't ease the pain. I look at him once again and I can tell that he is genuinely hurting, just like I am. I pull him up and we never lose eye contact. He bends his head down and silently asks to kiss me. He stops just millimeters away from my mouth. His breath caresses my lips and in this moment I want nothing more than his mouth on mine. "May I?" He's giving me a chance to deny him, but I no longer have the will.

I answer his request by wiping the tear away with my thumb and bringing his lips to mine. The kiss starts slow and passionate. His hand skims along my hip as he deepens the kiss. He nips my bottom lip before licking away the pain. I can feel his erection growing along my stomach. He lifts me up and I instinctively wrap my legs around his waist. He growls as I grind myself against his cock. Things are getting hot and heavy fast until my door swings open.

"I don't believe this shit. You're just going to let this motherfucker back in your good graces? God I never should have left you two alone. I knew once I no longer heard the arguing that you were forgiving him," Jordan screams. "I can't believe you Shiv," she whispers this time before walking out of the room shaking her head.

Grayson puts me down. "I think I better go," he says solemnly. "Why don't you come over this weekend so we can talk about where we go from here?" I find myself biting on the pad of my thumb. This is not good. Awkward tension fills the room. I don't want him to leave so soon, but I know Jordan and I need to talk. Her protective hackles are up and I must somehow smoothe this over. First, I must convey to Grayson that things will not be the way they were before.

"Whatever we decide, we need to go slow. I'm not going to be your fuck buddy again."

"You were never a fuck buddy," he says with air quotes. "But let's talk when there is not a threat of interruptions," he suggests.

There are so many questions that I need answered, but I agree to table them for now. I need to placate Jordan. Grayson gives me one last forehead kiss before heading out the door. As soon as he is gone, the wrath of Jordan is upon me.

She walks in with a cool exterior, but I'm not fooled. "I'm just going to say this and then I'm done."

"Jordan—," I begin, but I'm silenced immediately.

"Let me finish Shiv." She takes a deep breath before continuing. "I've watched two men destroy you in the course of one semester. You always say that your mother taught you that love is volatile, yet you subconsciously yearn to be loved. So much so that you take unnecessary risks."

"He says he loves me Jordan and I believe him. It's awful the way things transpired, but technically I had no claim to him."

"Damn, it's worse than I thought. You're rationalizing his behavior. Regardless of any title, he fucked someone else as soon as he dumped you. He showed you that you were easily replaceable. Only this time around will be much worse if you're in an actual relationship. He destroyed you before and you're giving him the opportunity to smash the remaining pieces of your sanity. You're giving him too much power to hurt you Shiv and I don't want any part of it. You're on your own." I am stunned stupid. I can't form one coherent sentence. I know there is truth to what she is saying, but it still hurts to hear it. She stomps out of my room and slams the door, betraying that cool facade she entered with.

Once she is gone, the damn breaks and my tears come in a rush. I turn off the music that had faded in the background and then crawl into bed. I cry my eyes out at the unfairness of it all.

I AM ANXIOUS this morning to discover what the dynamic of my relationship with Jordan will be. Has she calmed down? It's my life, damn it. After getting ready, I walk into the kitchen and see that she is sitting in the same spot she was yesterday morning. Except this time she isn't on the phone and there is no coffee made for me. I pop a k-cup of coffee in the Keurig and watch her as she keeps her back to me. So this is how she's going to play it—the silent treatment. After my coffee finishes brewing, I put it in my travel mug and go stand next to her. She doesn't acknowledge my presence. Instead she gets up and head out the door, leaving me no choice but to follow her so I don't get left behind. The car ride to school is silent and awkward. The tension lies thick in the air. I watch the traffic out of my passenger window so she doesn't see the tears that threaten to release. My face is hot with frustration that she is making me choose a side. Her non-verbalized ultimatum is as clear as writing on the wall. If I get involved with Grayson again, I will lose our friendship. She talks about the risk of Grayson hurting me again, yet she is doing a fine job all on her own.

When the car comes to a stop, I get out as fast as I can in this annoying boot and head towards my first class.

I'm heart-broken that my closest friendship is in the

toilet. I can't choose Grayson over her and she knows it. It's so unfair. I'm not allowed to see if we have a real shot to make things work? I resent that Jordan is trying to take my chance at happiness away from me. I know she thinks she is protecting me, but I didn't ask for her protection. Maybe I am making a huge mistake by letting Grayson back in, but isn't that for me to find out?

My three classes fly by in a haze. I've been distracted the whole day. I'm supposed to meet Jordan by the library since this is our meet up spot before driving home. I wonder if she will show up or will she leave me? She can't be that mad or could she? I reach the library and she is not here. Ten more minutes pass and I sink to the steps in defeat. A couple of tears trickle from my eyes before a pair of feet appear in front of me. I look up slowly and Jordan visibly finches at the sight of my tear stained face, but she stays quiet. I get up and follow her to the car. She puts music on to fill the silence this time and I'm thankful for the reprieve. My phone buzzes in my purse so I take it out, hoping that it is not Grayson. I see that I have a few missed calls from an unknown number and I freeze. I'm hesitant to open the text message just left, but I do anyway.

Unknown Caller: Welcome back Shiv!!! I see you're healing nicely. Did you like my little surprise with your tire?

My face blanches and my stomach twists. My phone stalker just confirmed that he or she was responsible for my accident. Even worse, he or she knows that I'm back and is definitely watching me. I start to hyperventilate as fear grips me and steals my breath.

"What is it Shiv?" Jordan breaks her silence once she senses something is wrong.

I still can't speak so I pass her the phone. I watch as she gasps in horror. She quickly whips the car around in a U-turn to head in the opposite direction. "We're going to the police right now."

I can only nod. The realization that someone is trying to kill me is sitting heavily on my chest and I can't breathe. Jordan takes us to the precinct where Officer Richards works since he already has knowledge of the case. We are in luck that he is working today. He attempts to trace the source of the text and call, but it only leads to a burner phone as he suspected. He explains there isn't much to go on until this sick fuck makes a move. There's not much the police can do. He knows how scared I am and promises that he will personally patrol our area to see if he notices anything—nothing official, but I'm still thankful. He gives me safety tips including avoid being alone and paying attention to my surroundings. He also thinks carrying mace might help me feel more secure. *Yeah, right. I'm scared shitless.* Jordan pats my shoulder as we head out of the police station and it is her fist initiation of warmness since she stormed out of my room yesterday.

The ride home is slightly awkward. I don't know if her concern means she is not mad at me anymore.

"I'm scared, Jor," I admit. "Who would want to hurt me?"

"I know and I am too. Hopefully Officer Richards patrolling our area will help him catch this crazy bastard. Do you think it's possible that is Vanessa?"

"I don't think so. I think the calls began before she knew about Grayson and me. Besides I don't think she's that crazy."

"I don't know. The jury is still out on that one. I'm not going to rule her out just yet. Well, at least I know you're safe as long as you avoid being alone." She lets out a deep breath and I just know she is about address the big ass elephant in the car. "We need to talk," she begins. "I said some harsh things to you yesterday, but I just felt so disappointed in your choice to let the man who nearly destroyed you have a second chance."

"Jordan, Grayson and I are not together. We still have a lot to discuss and even then I would want things to go slow this time." I sneak a peek at her from the corner of my eye. I tangle my fingers together in my lap and push forward. "I don't want to lose our friendship and I think you know I would never choose a man over you— well unless that man was my husband," I say smiling.

"I know and the same here. I don't want to make you choose. I just want you to be smart and not let your heart make the decisions for you. I don't ever want to see you so distraught again." She reaches over and untangles my hands and squeezes my hand in hers. "During our talks you always tell me how volatile love is and how you will never put up with the things your mother dealt with. Hell, Liam was kicked to the curb for his indiscretion and you moved on rather quickly. I'm just afraid Grayson's hold on you is so much stronger than you realize."

"Me and Grayson's arrangement was different. Neither one of us planned to take things as far as they went. He explained that he fell in love with me and didn't know what to do with that. I'm gathering he was burned the last time he fell in love so he did what a lot of men do—he ran." Jordan parks the car once we arrive at our condo and gives me her full attention. "The only reason I'm even considering going down that road again is because we weren't in a relationship or an arrangement either for that matter, when he slept with Vanessa. Still he has a lot explaining to do regarding the things Vanessa disclosed at the hospital."

Jordan nods her head in agreement and we head inside. I had told her everything over the holidays before she left to go on a retreat with her parents.

"Just tread lightly. Make him work for your affection. I was pissed yesterday, but you know I will always have your back."

"Thanks Jor. This whole fiasco has actually given me some time to reflect on what I want." I look her in the eyes so she can see my conviction. "I'm no longer willing to hide behind my parent's failed marriage. I refuse to use them as a measure of how love is or isn't. You have to work at it and you get what you accept. That being said, Grayson has his work cut out for him." I smile at my newfound introspection and Jordan smiles back at me.

"That is what I want to hear. It's all that I ask for." She seems satisfied with my reasoning so we change the subject. "So I heard from Trevor today. He'll be back in town this weekend. I can't wait to see him," she gushes. Trevor graduated this past December so he took an extended break during his visit home.

"That's good to hear. You guys may need to get a room for all the make-up-for-lost-time sex you're going to have. I definitely don't want the surround sound edition," I laugh.

"Me? You and professor lover boy are probably going to be getting it in with some hot make-up sex," she teases.

I playfully punch her in the arm. "I told you I wanted to go slow. I don't plan on having sex with him."

"That is what you say now until your unused vagina becomes alert to the carnal pheromones he will be putting off."

"Jordan, you are so retarded, you know that right?"

"You'll see." She starts taking out ingredients to cook and we settle into our familiar routine.

chapter
4

GRAYSON IS ON the way to pick me up and I'm a nervous wreck. Today we put all of our cards on the table. I'm afraid to let myself be vulnerable, but I'm going to tell him exactly how I feel and what I expect. I can't decide what to wear as evidenced by all the clothes I've pulled out of my dresser. Hell I was wearing a little of nothing when we last saw each other so I doubt he cares. I finally decide on a tank dress and ballet flats so I don't have to fight with this stupid boot on top of everything else. I have an appointment here in Los Angeles in a couple weeks to re-evaluate if I can get rid of the boot. I'm praying that is the case. I walk to my full-length mirror and I'm satisfied with my appearance. It doesn't scream sexy, but it's not that type of visit anyway. My red hair falls in waves just below my breasts. I had it cut some the day Jordan and I had a spa day. Grayson's assigned ringtone, Naughty Boy's *LaLaLa,* blares from my phone and I nearly trip over the clothes pile I have in the middle of my bedroom floor trying to get to it. The song ends before

I can answer. Grayson texts me immediately.

Grayson: I'm downstairs. Are you ready?

Me: Yep. I'll be down in a sec.

Jordan has already left to pick up Trevor from the airport so I won't see her before I leave.

I lock up and head toward the front our building. Grayson is waiting for me in the McLaren Sterling Moss I love so much. When he sees me approaching, he immediately gets out and opens my door for me. He crosses the front of the car to get back in and his eyes never leave mine. His stare is penetrating and intense. Once he closes his door he gives me that cocky smile I miss so much.

"You didn't bring an overnight bag," he says.

"Baby steps, Grayson. We have some talking to do before we can get to the overnight bag point." I hope my bravado doesn't give away how much his scent enclosed in this car is getting to me. He winks at me and starts the engine.

"Hmmm… Okay sweetheart. I'll follow your lead." I want to kiss that grin right off his face. Jordan wasn't kidding about the whole pheromone thing. His eyes are on the road and I use this time to steal small glances at him. The muscles in his arm flexes as he handle the steering wheel. I can see every cut of his delicious abs through his fitted tee. The thick column of his neck is even sexy. He runs his hand through his inky black locks and my eyes follow the gesture. His hair is slightly longer on top than before in that just fucked way. I imagine pulling his hair while he pounds me.

I bite my lip at the visual. He turns and looks at me and

I am hit with all that gorgeousness at once. He winks at me again and I know I've just been busted checking him out. I flush crimson. He lets out a soft chuckle at my embarrassment. I look away, determined not to be distracted by his sex appeal. Instead, I mentally prepare the questions I need answers to. I'm pulled out my reverie by the feel of his hand grasping my knee.

"What are you thinking about so hard about over there?"

"Just enjoying the view," I lie as I look into the distance. The view I want to see is causing me to become a horny mess.

"Hmmm, okay," he says. He gives my knee a squeeze before removing his hand. I immediately feel bereft. Looking once more out of the window, I see that we are leaving the city limits. What hotel are we going to? We take a series of turns, climbing higher in altitude as we drive along the mountainside.

"Grayson? Where are we going?"

"I'm taking you to my home. No more hotels. This is our beginning, if you let it be." He glances at me briefly for my reaction, but I'm stunned. This is a huge step. I don't how to process his one-eighty behavior so I keep quiet.

We finally pull up to his home and it is not even on the same scale of any of the hotels we stayed at.

This gem is a single story home overlooking all of Los Angeles. The sun is setting now so the solar lights illuminate the landscaped bamboo, palms, and exotic trees. It's location offers total seclusion, yet we're only about fifteen minutes from everything. He opens the door and I don't miss his subtle touch to my lower back as he guides me in. Heat sears my flesh from his fingertips. Our eyes meet and unspoken lust is evident between us.

"Let me give you the tour," he offers. "It's only three bedrooms, but it is enough space for me." I agree, but this place is definitely at odds with the penthouse he always rented. I knew he only wanted the extra space to ensure that he didn't have to share a bedroom with me.

"The view is gorgeous." Windows line the entire back of the house. I can see the romantic lit pool and I imagine the fun we can have in it with the seclusion.

"Yeah. You get a view of the city from every room. I love the natural light that this place gets during the day and the twinkle of the city lights at night."

"Well, I hope you have curtains in the bedroom. I won't be a fan of natural sunlight in the morning. I'm so not a morning person."

"Does that mean you're staying the night with me?" he says grinning. I avert my eyes from his as I realize my mistake.

"No. I was just making a blanket statement," I say waving him off.

"Well, let me show you the rest of the house." The wicked gleam in his eyes hints that he rather being doing something else. We step into the living room and the open space is a compilation of creams, browns, oranges, and yellows. Contemporary furnishings and decor complement the mid-century modern architecture. The two bedrooms feature an Asian decor with platform beds, bamboo sliding doors, and a Japanese styled bath in the master bedroom. This place is absolutely breath taking.

"I think we should head back to the living room. Having you in my bedroom for the first time is very distracting." He winks at me. "We won't get much talking done in here." He tucks a stray hair behind my ear before pulling me by the hand back into the living room.

"Are you hungry?" I take a seat and watch as he pours us a glass of some expensive-looking French wine.

"No. I'm okay for now." My stomach is suddenly in knots as we embark on this much needed talk.

He passes me a glass of the liquid courage and I am thankful. "Okay, let's talk. I can start if you want."

I nod my head in the affirmative. I need to gather my thoughts and let the wine soothe my nerves. I want answers, but I'm afraid of the outcome once I have them. Will we be able to move forward? He chooses to sit across from me and I'm glad. His nearness is distracting.

"Okay. As I said before, I fell in love with you. I think subconsciously I already knew. I started letting you in the moment I began going against my own norm. Having you sleep in my bed was huge for me. That last night we spent together was amazing. I confided in Vanessa the feelings that I was developing for you and she called bullshit. She accused me of manipulating my therapy." He takes a cleansing breath and looks me in the eyes. "Siobhan, I'm a sex addict. I'm currently in therapy, but she couldn't be more wrong. The minute I started defending my actions and feelings, I knew that I was deeply in love with you and it scared the shit out of me. Rather than run to you and beg you to take me back, I took the coward's way out. I fucked Vanessa and slept in the bed with her to prove to myself that my love for you was a lie. When I saw you at Bailey's the next day and your reaction to Vanessa's statement, it crushed me."

Tears stream down my face. I'm so overwhelmed right now. Oh. My. God. *He just admitted that he is a sex addict.* He tried to fuck me out of his system. The feelings from that day come back to me in a rush. He is at my side now, furiously trying to brush away the tears. "Please don't cry baby. I'm so sorry."

I push away from him and walk to the bar and refill my glass. "What do you mean you're a sex addict?"

I can't deal with thoughts of him and Vanessa right now. I gulp down the glass of wine I just poured and refill another. The wine is not doing its job fast enough. He walks over to me once again and grabs my hand. He eases the glass away from me. "Baby, we need to have this conversation sober. I know it hurts and for that I'm truly sorry. I will do everything in my power to never have to see this look in your eyes ever again." He tilts my chin up and kisses me softly. The kiss is brief, but it conveys his sincerity. "I was in love once before. Her name was Celeste and she was my fiancée."

A lump forms in my throat. It is hard to hear that someone else had his heart. "What happened with her? Did she break your heart? Is that why you're such a commitment phobe?" I fire rapid questions his way, but he doesn't seem deterred.

"Well, to make a long story short, my mother died of cancer when I was nine. My father had a couple women in his life before he met Vivian. Until her, I missed out on that mother figure. I grew up keeping girls at arms-length because of the role models my father paraded around with showed me women couldn't be trusted. I didn't trust the idea of love. I can still remember how much it hurt to watch my mother fade away." His eyes close as he reminisces on the memories. "I met Celeste my junior year in college and I fell for her instantly. I was ready to put my playboy ways aside. Ironically, it was Vanessa who introduced us. Celeste was her roommate."

"Vanessa mentioned that you two have been friends since she was eleven and you were thirteen. You never sought out a relationship with her?" Fourteen years is a very long time to have her hooks in him. No wonder they have such a strong bond.

"No. Our families are close and would like to see us together though." His uneasiness is apparent so I know there is more. "I'm going to be completely transparent right now so please remember this is my past and nothing more. Vanessa basically grew up with Bailey and I because our parents were so close, but we didn't start having sex until she arrived as a freshman at USC. She knew I wasn't looking for anything beyond sex. She was completely fine with it because she was doing her own thing as well. When she introduced me to her roommate Celeste, she never thought things would progress past a casual hook up. I had no control over how hard I fell for this girl. We dated for a year before I proposed. We were only engaged for a few months before her horrible car accident."

Holy shit. This must be the reference Vanessa was speaking of when she commented about the significance of my accident. *Damn.* "Did she die?"

"No, but our love did." He sees the confusion on my face so he continues. "She was hospitalized for several weeks, in a coma. When she regained consciousness, she had no recollection of our relationship or me. Her long-term memory was intact so she remembered her family, but I was a stranger to her. The doctors were unsure if she would ever regain those memories. We tried to work things out, but we grew apart. She eventually fell in love with someone else and I was devastated.

Pieces of his conversation in the hall with Vanessa that day are starting to make sense. He has had such bad luck with love, I can see why he is scared to allow himself to feel for someone. With my own experiences, I can relate. I'm scared to ask this next question, but I know that I have to. "Grayson, are you still in love with her?" He runs a hand through his hair and lets out a deep breath. He closes his eyes and shakes his head no as though he's never thought about this until now. When opens his eyes, they hold mine. His smile is sad and it is evident that that she is still a sore topic for him.

"Honestly, she will always hold a special place in my heart because she was my first love. But to answer your question, no I'm not in love with her. Six years has passed. The scars are there though. This is where my addiction comes in. I used sex to numb the memory of her. I fucked countless women as an escape from the pain— careful not to let anyone else get too close. Vanessa and I continued to mess around in between our own hook ups, but then she told me I needed to seek help for my dependency. I told her she was fucking crazy at first and then I realized she was right."

"You said 'used' as in past tense. What about now?" Having a glimpse into his past helps me understand his reservations, but I still hate his connection to that tramp and her influence with him.

"Well now, I have someone that I'm absolutely in love with and I'm not interested in sex with anyone else. You're my cure baby."

"Uh huh," I say with my own reservations. I don't want to be the healing balm to soothe his broken heart. I want to be the love of his life.

"Come here. I know that was a lot to hear, but please know that it is you that I want." He pulls me to him and my body melts into him. He uses his hands to tilt my face up to him and this time the kiss is not soft or comforting. It is raw and hungry. His tongue seeks entrance and I let him in. His hands slide under my dress and my panties pool with wetness. "Please tell me you're mine now, baby. I need to hear it."

I don't hesitate. We have a long way to go and a lot of healing to do, but I can't deny this man. "I'm yours."

He growls his approval before ripping my panties off. He picks me up and I have no choice but to hang on for the ride as he makes determined strides toward the bedroom. "There's no turning back baby. I'm going to fuck you so hard. Fuck zero or anything else in between. Sixty is what you're getting so I hope you're ready," he says in reference to his previous comment about not taking me from zero to sixty without incremental exposure. *Fuck, I'm ready for sixty.* He slides my dress over my head and undoes my bra. He stands back and takes me in like I'm his last meal. I fight the urge to cover myself. I let him have his fill. He begins to remove his own clothes and holy hell, I forgot just how Adonis-like his body was. Don't get me wrong, he's starred in my recent fantasies, but they have nothing on the real thing. I lick my lips as he stalks toward me with a smirk. His hardness is standing at attention, nearly touching his navel. The vein that runs along the dorsal side adds to its virile perfection. The thickness intimidates me. He grabs my hand and wraps it around the head. He glides my hand over him and I can feel him hardening even more. I try to swallow the lump in my throat.

chapter 5

"YOU MISS MY cock baby?" He winks at me and I squeeze my legs together to stave off the ache that is rolling through my sex. Grayson crawls to me and pries my legs apart. "Uhh-huh, open your legs for me. I want to see how wet you are."

"Still crass as ever I see." I secretly love how filthy his mouth is. It gets me so hot.

"Always love. You haven't seen anything yet." He nibbles at my inner thigh and I let my head fall back on the bed. He grips my hips in his arms and uses his hold to keep me still as he swipes his skilled tongue across my clit. I nearly buck off the bed. His licks are slow, controlled, and torturous. He makes little swirls with his tongue that should be illegal. "Fuck, you have such a gorgeous pussy. I can stay right here and devour your sweetness all day." He sucks on my clit with such fervor. He inserts one finger and then two, stretching me. I moan and thrash about. It's too much. He tightens his grip to hold me still and continues his assault. He tongues me deep and it has me grabbing his hair as I buck my hips. I think I'm going to pass out when the first wave of ecstasy rolls through me. My legs tremble around his head, but he doesn't stop. He begins nibbling at my bud alternated with a lethal swirl of his talented tongue. I pull on his hair as I ride out my second orgasm. *Shit he's still licking me.*

"Grayson, please." My legs clamp around his head as he brings me once again to the brink of another orgasm. Damn, I didn't know I could come so many times just from oral sex.

"There it is. That is what I was waiting to hear. I want you begging. I want your tight little pussy good and wet because once I sink my cock into you baby, after all these weeks, I won't be able to hold back." His filthy words send me right over the edge. He grabs the condom that he had thrown on the bed and I watch as he rolls it over his thickness. *God, I hope he still fits.* He stands up bringing me with him as he picks me up. "I love these gorgeous fucking legs wrapped around my waist and your pussy wrapped around my cock. I've missed this so much." His hands grasp my outer thighs as he lifts me slightly. He lowers me slowly onto the length of his cock and I begin to stretch to take every delicious inch. It feels so good that I'm already anticipating the ride. Once I'm fully seated, he gives me a moment to adjust to his fullness. I attempt to lift my hips to start us off, but he kisses me instead. His lips caress mine as he explores my mouth. I can taste myself on his tongue. His hands tangle in my hair as he deepens the kiss. I am free falling. He grinds himself against me and I whimper with need.

"What's wrong baby?" He reaches further down and massages my ass. I can't tear my eyes away from his. "Are you ready for this," he says while angling his hips in an upward thrust.

"Damn it, Grayson. Fuck me already!" He chuckles at my frustration.

"Whatever you want love." He pulls out and inches back in me slowly and I can feel myself stretching even more to accommodate his girth. The feeling is heavenly. He begins sucking on my neck and the combined feeling is almost more than I can handle. "Your pussy missed me baby. It's gripping my cock so hard." He slides in to the hilt once again and stills to let me reacclimatize to his size.

The wiggle of my hips is the only sign he needs to spur along. He bounces me on his cock—the first few strokes are slow and I meet him stroke for stroke. I know the instant his control snaps because he starts pounding me harder. His hips piston with each increasing stroke. I hold on for the ride as he impales me. His balls slap against me as he finds a way to go deeper. "Damn, I've missed this pussy," he swears. His arms work double time as he uses his strength to bounce me on his impressive erection. My walls clamp down on him as I come hard and in turn milk his release. He growls in pleasure. We both bask in how amazing that just was. Our pants are in sync. He peels off the used condom before he lowers me to bed and begins sucking on my breasts.

"I've missed these too," he says as he nips at one of nipples.

"So you only missed my body," I tease.

"I miss everything that you are babe." *Nice save.* I can feel him getting hard again. Oh my. He flips us over and now I'm on top. I briefly worry about my ability to ride in this position, but my doubt is replaced by his grip on my hips and him bouncing me on his dick. Once again, he's got this. He sets the pace and watches as my tits bounce in time with the rhythm he has set. It's not long before I find my own rhythm as I grind down on him between stokes. Shit. I'm not going to last. I throw my head back and scream his name as the stars dance behind my eyes.

"Fuck, that is the hottest thing I've ever seen," he says as he finds his own release. He turns me on my side and I think we're about to cuddle. *Wrong.* He peels off the used condom and then wraps his leg on top of mine. He begins to fondle my now tender breasts. "I love watching you come. That shit is so fucking hot. I'm going to enjoy watching this look on your face all night. I have a lot of making up to do."

I never said I was staying the night, but who am I kidding. This man has just given me five orgasms with promise of more to come. I'm not going anywhere. I smile at my inner dialogue.

"That's what I thought," he smirks.

"You're pretty sure of yourself back there," I say as he massages my hip.

"No, baby. I'm just listening to your body and it is demanding that I fuck you some more." To emphasize his point, he runs his dick along the crease of my ass. Good god. He is already hard again. I look over my shoulder at him and he gives me the most wicked grin. "I told you I had a lot of making up to do. I wasn't kidding. This pussy will be sore tomorrow, but I will lick it better." He lifts my leg slightly and slides into me from behind. Again his strokes are slow and deliberate. His hands find my breast and he twirls my nipples through his fingertips. I back my ass into him to meet his strokes and he lets out a guttural growl. He pounds into me harder and I love it. I reach back and pull his hair.

"Shit, what are you doing to me Siobhan?" He plunges into me one last time and we're both falling over the edge. He slaps my ass and rubs it. "I love you baby. I will spend however long it takes showing you just how much."

I know our talk is far from over. There is still so much I need to know, but we had a good start. I roll over on my back and watch this beautiful man stare down at me.

"Are you hungry now?"

"Yes," I grin. He has worked up my appetite.

He jumps out of the bed and throws on his boxers. He picks up his T-shirt and slips it over my head. His scent lingers on the fabric and is intoxicating. "Come on. Let me cook you something." I twist my hair before winding it in a bun. Grayson looks over at me and frowns. He walks over to me and undoes my messy bun. "Leave it wild baby. Your hair is so sexy. I wanted to pull it like you were pulling mine while I fucked you."

"Hmmm."

"Hmmm, what?"

"You could have. I think that would've been hot. I kind of wanted you to." I flush crimson at my admission. I cover my face, but he pulls my hands away.

"Don't ever be afraid to voice what you want in the bedroom love. Tell me what you like. I already know that you like my filthy mouth," he smirks. "But I don't want to always guess. Take what you want from me. I'm into some kinky shit so you can't surprise me."

"Kinky eh? Like what?" The wine coursing through my blood is long gone, so I'm going to have to be bold on my own.

"I rather show you," he says pulling me to him. He licks

my lips before pulling away. "But let's eat first." *I never knew he was such a tease.*

"Tease," I accuse.

"Never that baby. I plan to fuck you again as soon as we finish eating. I'm just afraid that if I pull out all my kinky debauchery, you'll run," he smiles.

"What happened to sixty?" I challenge.

"Baby my brand of kink is beyond sixty. I don't even know if it can be quantified on a scale," he warns. "Sixty is just an expression of getting you out of your shell so you'll enjoy the regular sex you haven't been exposed to. When I turn it up a notch, you'll know."

My sex clinches at the possibility. "I can handle anything you dish out."

"We'll see. For now let me make you my famous spaghetti." I follow him to the kitchen and sit at the counter as he makes the preparations. He pours me a glass of wine and I watch in amazement as he chops the mushrooms and parsley. He even makes cooking look sexy. After the all the prep work is done, the noodles are put to boil. He saunters over to me and lifts me out of my chair. He sets me on the counter and starts his assault on my lips. The kiss is tender and slow. He raises the T-shirt up and places a tiny kiss to my nipple. One and then the other. He pulls one into his mouth and begins to suck. A whimper slips past my lips and he smiles. He pulls away and I tighten my grip around his waist to keep him in place.

"Tease," I accuse again.

"Just keeping you warm. I want your pussy to be ready for me when we finish eating."

He pulls away and this time I let him go.

I have a plan. *Payback is a bitch. I'll teach him to tease me*. I finish my wine and pour myself another glass. Okay so, I'm going to need just a little liquid courage for this plan. I wait until he carries our plates of spaghetti to the dinner table. I slip off his shirt and walk over to the table naked. His eyes nearly bulge out of his head when he turns around and sees me. He quickly puts our plates down, but I take a seat. I can see his erection protruding from his boxers. When he is close enough to me, I use my sitting position to my advantage. I pull his hard cock out from his boxers. He hisses at my touch. I lick the tip before taking the head into my mouth. I suck him slowly as my hand massages his balls. His head falls back and his eyes close in ecstasy. He grabs my hair, ready for me to take him deeper. My devious smile forms around his cock as I pull back and tuck him back into his boxers.

"What the hell?" He looks down at me confused.

"I'm just keeping you warm baby. Turnabout is fair play love," I say using his words on him.

"Touché. But you do know that you will be paying for that little stunt?" He reluctantly takes his seat and I snicker. "Laugh it up now baby. I have something special in mind for you." I laugh harder. It may be short lived, but it feels good for now to beat him at his own game.

"We eat our spaghetti and I must admit that it is absolutely delicious. He stares across the table at me and I can see the lust in his eyes. *Oh. God*. I've really poked the bear. He looks ready to pounce at any minute. I get up to bring my plate to the kitchen and I'm grabbed from behind. He throws me over his shoulder fireman style before he takes the plate out of my hand. He places it in the sink and heads towards the bedroom. He slaps my ass and I let out a squeal. He pushes the door close with his foot and then he does something unexpected. He lifts me up higher and secures my legs around his head. He walks forward until my back rests against the door. He buries his face in my pussy and begins his lovely torment. He sucks on my nub with renewed fervor. My hips are unable to buck in this position so he is in total control. I squeeze my legs tighter, but he just pries them apart and continues his punishment. His tongue plunges inside me and I cry out my pleasure.

He looks up at me with that smirk I love so much. "You were saying baby?" I'm boneless. He walks us over to the bed, but I'm spent. He slides up between my legs and begins nibbling on my neck. "Are you still on the pill?" Fine time for him to ask now, but I nod yes so he can bury himself deep inside me. He pushes me to two more orgasms before we both finally let exhaustion take us under.

THE CHIRPING OF my phone indicating I have an awaiting message pulls me from my slumber. Grayson's side of the bed is empty. I wrap the sheet around my naked frame and sit up to listen to my voicemail. Maybe he's out getting us breakfast. One second into the message and I sigh. Jordan was right. "Hey hooker. I knew Mr. Sexy Pants was going to lay it on you the minute he got you alone. You didn't stand a chance, really. Lost time and all that. Anyway, I stayed the night with Trevor so no worries. I'll see you Sunday." I shake my head as I end the call. She called it, yet I can't complain. My limbs and vagina are deliciously sore. I'm smiling stupidly at my phone when Grayson walks in wearing nothing but pajama bottoms. I ogle him from his sexy bare feet to his washboard abs. The light dusting of hair that travels south from his navel and disappears into his waistband has me licking my lips.

"Are you done eye fucking me?" he teases.

"I…" I can't even finish that lie. I so was. I cover my head with the sheet wrapped around me. God, I can't help that he is so hot. He has managed to turn me into walking hormones. I don't even recognize this insatiable version of myself. I feel Grayson's firm grip wrap around my left ankle before I'm being pull to the edge of the bed.

I squeal as I pull the sheets with me. He untangles me and throws me over his shoulder before heading toward the kitchen. "Oh. My. God. You psycho, please give me something to wear."

He slaps my bare ass and the sting causes moisture to pool between my legs. "Nope. You want to eye fuck me then I get to return the sentiment except I don't want clothes in the way," he smirks. "Now let me make us some breakfast baby." He puts me down on a stool at the kitchen counter. I fold my arms across my breasts.

"Oh, so you're a pycho and a comedian. A psychotic comedian, I sure can pick 'em." He throws his head back and belts out the sexiest laugh I've ever heard. "Grayson, I need my boot and a T-shirt please."

He quirks an eyebrow at me and gives me a wicked smile. "No boot means you can't leave that spot to get something to cover up," he laughs.

"Oh you just watch me, smart ass." I slide off the stool, but Grayson is quick. He halts my efforts and places me back on the stool.

"Stop baby before re-injure your ankle. I'm just teasing you because I feel like we've taken a couple steps backwards with your shyness. I just saw all of you last night, yet you still cover up." He smiles as he shakes his head, but he leaves to get me a shirt and my boot. Being completely naked is so different outside of sex. I don't want him to see my flaws compared to his perfection. When he returns, he lifts my right foot and takes my big toe into his mouth. He applies a light suction before continuing on to each toe. He gives me a flirtatious smile when he reaches the last one combined with a naughty wink that is just for me. "I love all of you baby. You are so perfect to me, from the top of your head to your sexy little toes. I'll give you the shirt you asked for, but know that your body was made for me and mine for you. I wouldn't change a thing." He hands me the T-shirt before slowly putting my boot on. His eyes never leaves mine. My heart melts at the tenderness he is showing. I can only nod, but it is enough. He kisses me lightly. I can't promise that I'll overcome my insecurities overnight, but for him, I'll try.

chapter
6

AFTER BREAKFAST, GRAYSON and I spend the day lounging around. We banter with ease and the rounds of marathon sex are explosive. I didn't think I could fall any harder for this man, but I was wrong. We have a lot of mending to do, but I'm ready to try. We didn't speak much about Vanessa yesterday, but I need to know where she stands in his life. We sit here now lying on his sofa watching Netflix movies on his insanely expensive entertainment system. My head is in his lap and I'm enjoying his tender strokes down my arm.

"What's on your mind babe?" His hand stops and he looks down at me. His cerulean blue eyes pierce me. He is so perceptive to my feelings that it's bewildering sometimes.

"Just thinking."

"I can tell you're not here with me. You have that faraway look in your eyes." He bends down and kisses me on the temple. "This go round we have to communicate sweetheart. Let me know what's on your mind. What's bothering you?"

Okay here it goes. "Are you and Vanessa still friends?" I ask with air quotes around the friends. They sure did a lot of fucking to say they were supposed to be friends. Grayson pulls me up and onto his lap.

"Oh baby, please know that you have nothing to worry about. I don't know what Vanessa told you that day in your hospital room and I choose not to press the issue. If you want to share, I'm listening, but as far as I'm concerned we are moving forward. Understand this. She filled a void.

"We were two consenting adults that knew the score. I've never had these kind of feelings for her. We were great friends from childhood that called each other out on our bullshit and talked about our conquests." It doesn't get past me that he said 'were great friends.' "She was almost like one of the guys, but with a vagina," he finishes.

He didn't answer my original question. "But are you two still friends?"

"Our friendship is strained right now. I will never just abandon her if she was truly in need, but it will never be the way it was. She crossed a line. We still see each other at family gatherings or business ventures, but I don't seek her out. I told her this week at our family dinner that I was going to try to get you back—that I was in love with you. I choose us baby." His declaration brings a smile to my face. "Oh, and my father and Vivian want me to bring you to Sunday brunch tomorrow," he says sheepishly. Holy crap, this is huge. This means he told them about me.

"I don't know what to say. Do they know I'm the same person that came to dinner with Jordan a while back?"

"Yes. I told them everything. They know that you were

my student. They frowned on this, but they want to get to know you. I think the fact that you're no longer my student is easier to digest." He looks at me intently waiting for my answer

"Okay, but I need to go home and get some clothes. You can pick me up in the morning." I watch as his face contorts into confusion."You're going home now?"

"Yes. It's for the best. I need to catch up on some homework due next week. Besides, some time apart will prevent you from feeling claustrophobic," I assure. I get up to gather my things and he follows me into the bedroom.

"Nonsense. We've had a whole month of space. I need you in my bed. Naked and ready for my cock." He grabs me from behind and grinds his erection against my ass.

"You have a filthy mouth, you know that?" My head falls back against his shoulder as he digs his fingers into my hips.

"Yes. And you love the filth that comes out of my mouth." He reaches down and runs a finger through my folds. "Look at how wet you are for me." He pulls us both over to the bed and bends me over. He slides in me from behind and I whimper.

"Shit Grayson. You feel so good."

"Take all of me. Feel me marking what's mine." He grabs my hair in his fist and pounds me relentlessly. My knees weaken with each powerful stroke so he wraps his other hand around my waist to hold me up. He explodes inside me and I'm right there with him. We fall onto the bed and he pulls me close to him.

"Stay with me tonight baby. I promise to bring you home in time to get clothes in the morning."

I couldn't move even if I wanted to. "Okay," I say simply. I watch as a grin spreads across his sexy lips. I melt into his hold and snuggle my head against his chest. His breath evens out and I know he has fallen asleep. *A day of marathon sex will do that to you.* I close my eyes in contentment that I have the love of this beautiful man.

"GET UP SWEETHEART. We need to stop by your place before we head to brunch with my parents." I wake up to Grayson leaning over me smiling. He has the curtain wide open to let the sunlight filter through. The early morning rays reflect in his captivating eyes making them appear even lighter. He leans down even further and kisses me. I don't even care that I haven't brushed yet, this man is so freaking addicting.

"Uh-uh baby. You keep kissing me like that and we won't make it out of this bed," he says pulling away. "I put a shirt and some shorts over there on the chair until we get to your place. It will be swimming on you, but it's all I have."

"It'll be fine." When he gets out of the bed, I see his erection as he strolls to the bathroom. He is so comfortable with his nudity. I hear him turn on the shower so I get up to gather my things. I guess it's best that we didn't shower together. I'm really sore today. Every move I make is a reminder of our sex filled weekend.

When we arrive at my place, there is no sign of Jordan. She must still be at Trevor's. Damn, I could really use her advice on what to wear. Grayson takes a seat in the living room and turns on the television while I get ready. I must try on a gazillion outfits, looking for a suitable meet-the-parents look. Trouble is, I don't know what the hell I'm looking for. I definitely don't possess the sophistication or upper crust background that Vanessa does. I look at the pile of clothes on my bed and I want to scream in frustration. I'm on my way to look in Jordan's closet when Grayson appears in the doorway. His eyes widen at the clothes infested vomit that is my room.

"Babe, it's been thirty minutes. What are you doing?" I roll my eyes because isn't it obvious? I wave my hand at all the clothes on the bed and on the floor causing him to take another look at the mess I've created.

"I don't have anything to wear," I huff.

That grin I love so much spreads across his face. "That's a lot of clothes over there to be nothing."

He doesn't understand my wardrobe meltdown. "I'm going to go look in Jordan's closet." I don't get far. He wraps his hands around my waist and kisses me on the temple.

"You're over thinking this baby. Don't be nervous. My parents are going to love you. Come on, let's find you something here in all these clothes you pulled out."

The first thing he picks up is a body con dress that I wore the night we first danced at Drai's Hollywood. Oh. My. God. His parents will think I'm a skank for sure. "Grayson, I'm not wearing that. You want my ass on display for your family?"

"I really love your ass baby. It's so round and perfect. I want to take a bite out of it right now," he teases.

"Grayson!" I'm glad that he likes the size of my ass, but I'm sure his parents won't be equally impressed.

"Just kidding love—not about your ass though." He picks up a grey long sleeved baby doll dress and pairs it with the grey and black striped tights I have lying on the bed. Why didn't I see this combo? It's sad that even his fashion sense is better than mine. He smiles at his accomplishment and pats me on the ass. "I will be seeing this ass later, but for now, get dressed." He plops on my bed and leans back like he is waiting for the show. I feel self-conscious about him watching me and he knows it, but I push past my embarrassment. I undress with my back to him trying to pretend he's not in the room.

"Beautiful," he whispers. *Yeah, so much for pretending.*

WHEN WE PULL up to the mansion, my nerves materialize. What if they don't like me? Grayson opens my door and helps me out of the car. I didn't even realize he had already gotten out. "We'll go around back. We're having brunch in the garden," he says. We take several steps down into the enchanting greenery before following a stone path to a gazebo.

The bouquet of the various flowers in bloom is heavenly. The statues and fountains add to the beauty of the grounds. As we near the table where his parents are sitting, my heart stops and a lump forms in my throat. Grayson feels the tension in our connected hands and follows my gaze. Vanessa is sitting to the right of Vivian.

"What the fuck?" he mumbles. Hi jaw ticks and his anger is evident. "Vivian, why is she here?" he scolds. Vivian is silenced by the wave of Vanessa's hand.

"Sorry if I'm intruding Grayson. Vivian didn't invite me. It's been a while since I've come over for Sunday brunch and I wanted to visit. That's all. I didn't know you'd be here or that you'd have company. I can go if you want," Vanessa explains solemnly.

"Bullshit. You know that the odds were likely that I'd be here. Siobhan is not company either, she's my girlfriend. You don't have to leave because we're going." He looks at me apologetically, silently pleading with me not to be upset. "Let's go baby."

Vivian's seat scrapes against the pavement as she gets up. She is visibly worried that brunch is ruined. "You don't have to leave son."

"I'll go," Vanessa offers. I don't want this bitch to think her presence bothers me or ruin brunch.

"It's okay Grayson. I'm fine with her being here. She's here to visit with your parents. I know I have nothing to worry about."

The snarl on her face is fleeting, but not fast enough. She can pretend she doesn't care that I'm here with Grayson or the fact that he just announced me as his girlfriend, but I know better. *Take that bitch. He's mine.* Let her sit through this brunch while I enjoy time with my man. Grayson looks skeptical, but he surprises me by pulling me in for a kiss right in front of everyone. Nothing obscene, but I still flush crimson at the public display of affection. "Are you sure baby?" He looks at me intently, looking for any sign of wavering thoughts.

"I'm sure." I squeeze his hand and he seems appeased for now. He pulls out a seat for me on his father's side of the table. Surprisingly, he had been silent through this whole ordeal. Grayson takes a seat next to me, which means we are sitting across from Vanessa and Vivian. She looks a little too polished for morning brunch in her form fitting dress and heels. *Didn't know Grayson would be here my ass. Lying skank.* God, I can't stand her.

"So Siobhan, how are your classes this semester? You're

getting ready to graduate, right?" Grayson's father's questioning snaps me out of my inner Vanessa-hating monologue.

"That's right Mr. Michaels. I'm looking forward to it."

"You can call me Ben dear. No need for formalities here with us." A lady who looks to be in her mid-forties wheels over a cart with several dome covered plates.

She places each of them on the table before uncovering the feast. There is so much food. An assortment of meats, fruits, waffles, pastries, and more makes my mouth water. Grayson pours me a mimosa before making himself one. From the corner of my eye I can see the grimace that Vanessa is trying so desperately trying to hide.

"What does the university policy say about dating students, son? I know she is no longer 'your' student, but is it allowed?" Ben is straight to the point. And there it is. The turning point of this lovely meal. I just lost my appetite. I fidget in my seat and Grayson notices. He stills my bouncing leg with a gentle caress.

"Seeing as though the university is your alma mater dad, I know you're aware it's not allowed," Grayson accuses.

"I am. I just wanted to make sure that you were aware. What are your plans son? Surely, you can't be seen publicly. This has to be a strain on such a new relationship."

"We'll manage. In four shorts months, it will be a non-issue." He leans over and kisses me on the temple. "Get what you want baby," he says as he loads his plate with various fixings. Ben huffs under his breath, but then proceeds to make his own plate. Vanessa of course, only puts a few pieces of fruit on her plate. Vivian eyes us a moment before she chimes in with what I feel will be another attack.

"So what are your plans after graduation, Siobhan?

Grayson tells us you're a business major." The snarky grin on Vanessa's face tells me she is enjoying this little inquisition.

"Well I make handmade soap so I was thinking of starting my own business selling natural handmade products," I smile.

"Have you written out a business plan? Dreams are fine dear until it's time to enter the real world where you'll have bills. Dreams don't pay those," she laughs. "Maybe Vanessa can help you with planning. She works with Grayson at his father's company so she has a lot of valuable knowledge." The smirk on Vanessa's face is almost too much as she nods in the affirmative. Vivian just managed to make me feel unworthy of Grayson in one sentence. The premise was always there, she just brought it to the forefront. It's obvious that she would rather him be with Vanessa. Ben doesn't approve either. Why the fuck did they ask Grayson to bring me here? Was it to show me how much I don't belong in their world? Tears sting behind my eyes, but I refuse to let them fall. My skin burns hot as I try to get a handle on my emotions.

"Enough," Grayson booms. "This is not a fucking social visit, it's a god damn attack and I will not stand for it!"

"Watch your mouth son," Ben warns. Grayson gets up so fast his chair falls to the pavement. He pulls me up and apologizes.

"I'm so sorry baby. This was a fucking set up and I wouldn't have brought you here had I known." He turns and lets them all have it. "Siobhan is who I want in my life. She's who I love. Get. The. Fuck. Over. It."

"She's not Celeste, Grayson," Vivian chastises. He clinches his fist a few times, but he doesn't bother to answer. Instead he grabs my hand and we head to the car.

chapter
7

THE SILENCE IN the car is deafening. The scene at brunch is on replay in my mind and this time, I can't stop the tears from falling. I try to quickly swipe them away, but Grayson catches me.

"Fuck!" he yells. He whips the car onto the shoulder of the road so fast, I startle. "Damn. I'm so fucking sorry baby. Please don't let their stupidity upset you." I turn to look out the window. I can't look at him right now. I don't want him to see the insecurity that is wreaking havoc on my psyche. I wipe my eyes with both hands now— desperate to keep my tears at bay.

"They want Vanessa for you," I stutter. I hate that I'm an insecure mess right now. Grayson gets out of the car and slams the door. He is on my side and opening my door before I can realize what he's doing. "Get out of the car Siobhan," he says too calmly. Where is he going with this? His no nonsense demeanor has me doing exactly as he asked.

"A little theatrical, don't you think?"

"God damn it," he swears as he kicks his tire. "You think I'm theatrical? Maybe a little insane? Fuck I feel like they just cause us to take more steps backwards. Baby, I asked you to get out of the car so I can look you in the eyes when I tell you this *again*. I. Love. You. I don't give a flying fuck what Vivian and my dad want. You're the one I want in my life so please don't punish me for this," he pleads. Of course he's right. He stood up to his parents for me. Hell, he was ready to go the minute he saw Vanessa, but I insisted on staying. I'm the one overreacting. I'm pissed at the situation, not at him. He has done nothing but shown me he loves me. He has changed so much of who he is for me already. I reach up and wrap my arms around his neck. I nod to let him know that we're okay, still too emotional over the whole ordeal. Grayson leans his head against mine and breathes a sigh of relief. "I love you baby," he says again in a gentle whisper. He presses me against the car and nibbles on my lips, coaxing me to open for him. His tongue slips in and he deepens the kiss. His hands slide under my dress and he palms my ass. And just like that, the bullshit with his parents and Vanessa is a fleeting memory. I forget that we're on the side of the highway for a second until a trucker honks his approval.

"Grayson people can see us," I say, trying to push him away.

"Hmmm, they can," he says slipping a finger between the fabric of my panties. "You're wet love. I think you secretly like the idea. Well, your body does anyway." I slap his shoulder in mock exasperation.

"We're not going to give the entire city of Los Angeles a peep show," I giggle.

"Well not the entire city," he grins wickedly as he in-serts a finger inside me. I clinch around his finger. "Let's get you home baby before I'm tempted to fuck you right here. I know you're not ready for exhibitionism yet."

"What do you mean I'm not ready *yet*? Are you into that?" *Holy shit.*

"Let's discuss it at a later time. You're getting my dick excited at the possibility." He nudges his erection against my hip for emphasis. "Just know, I plan on showing you what it feels like to orgasm in public. Nobody will be the wiser, but the risk will make your orgasm just that much more explosive," he promises.

My mouth gapes in shock. He truly is a freak. Could I ever be that bold with him? "Come on, I'll get you home so you can do those homework assignments you needed to do." When we get back to the condo, I think he is going to drop me off, but he surprises me by coming up. When we walk in, Jordan is cuddled up with Trevor watching tele-vision, but she lifts a questioning eyebrow at me. Grayson and I head straight to my bedroom.

"Are you hungry? You didn't get chance to eat any-thing?" My stomach picks this time to answer with a growl and he laughs. "Rest baby, I'll be back." He pulls back the covers on my bed and I don't argue. Between the marathon sex and confrontation at his parents' place, I'm feeling a lit-tle tired. I remove my boot and dress before crawling into bed. It doesn't take long for sleep to take me.

WHEN I WAKE up, the sun has set and Grayson is next to me in the bed reading the *Los Angeles Times*. The soft light from the bedside lamp gives me an award-winning view of his hard lines etched to perfection. He's not aware that I'm awake yet so I get to stare at this beautiful specimen sitting in my bed. His attentiveness and affection have taken a complete one-eighty. This man owns me completely. I hope he doesn't shatter my heart because broken is not even an option at this point. He would do irreparable damage.

He turns and catches me ogling him. "Eye fucking me again, babe?" He smiles as he pulls me to him. "I cooked you lunch, but you were asleep by the time I finished so I just let you sleep."

"You cooked? Where was Jordan?" This can't be good if she got her nosey hooks in him.

"It was fine baby. I asked if it was okay for me to use the kitchen. Trevor stuck around for a bit. I found ingredients to make chicken fajita wraps so he ate before leaving. Really nice guy. Jordan and I were able to bond over our common interest of cooking. We had a nice long talk about my past and my feelings for you. I think we turned the corner. You have a really good friend in her. She really loves you and has your best interests at in mind" he laughs. "She laid down the law and told me that she will have my balls if I hurt you again. I'm not really an open book about things that are personal, but I felt that it was important for her to understand my actions. No excuses baby. Just wanted to impart my own personal struggle to be a better man for you. For us."

I don't know what to say. I'm speechless over the extent he is taking to clear the path for us. He understands how important she is to me. This makes me love him even more. "Thank you for that. She is very important to me. I want the two most important people in my life, besides my parents to get along." My relationship with my dad is a strange one. We don't talk as much since he's busy traipsing around the world, picking up freelance photography work along the way. But when we do get a chance to talk, he always has so much to share with me about his adventures. He's invited me to join him when I finish my studies, but I don't plan on taking him up on it. I snap out of my wandering thoughts to find Grayson just smiling at me.

"You're important to me too love. When I do give a woman my heart, I love hard. So be very afraid," he kids. He's making a joke out of his feelings for me, but I can see the underlying sincerity in his eyes. He grabs my boot off the floor and begins putting it on my foot. He picks up his T-shirt off the floor and slides it over my head. "Come now woman. Let's see if there's any chicken wraps left while I fix you dinner."

"Wow. You're going to cook again. You must be working to get some," I tease.

"Baby, I don't have to work for that, it already belongs to me. I just want to spoil my woman. Oh, and I may have been warned about the extent of your cooking skills," he smirks. I'm going to kill Jordan. How dare she bash my cooking? I can make enough to get by. *Humph, I'll show him*.

"I can cook and I'm going to do just that. Be prepared to be amazed." We head into the kitchen, but there is no sign of Jordan. The door to her room is open and the light is off so I know that she is gone. "Sit down and relax babe." He smiles at my endearment or may be the fact that I'm cooking for him. I pull out a couple of wine glasses. It's not the good stuff that he has, but good enough. I pour us a glass of merlot while I get the ingredients together for my just-thought-of meal.

I find queso blanco Velveeta cheese and I fist pump at my yummy find. I grab the rye bread from the pantry and lightly spray the skillet with coconut oil. I open a can of tomato soup and pour it in a pot to heat up before continuing on with my deluxe grilled cheese sandwich.

"Smells delicious baby."

"It's not the stuff that you and Jordan make, but it's my version of a gourmet grill cheese sandwich with tomato soup." He takes a small sip of his wine and then stalks over to me.

"I rather eat you instead," he says nibbling on my ear. I turn my back to him because I need to watch my grilling.

"Grayson, you're going to make me burn our meal and then you're going to blame it on my cooking," I whine. He wraps his arms around my waist from behind.

"Just taking notes love." *Yeah right. As if.*

"Ummm hmmm. I'm sure you need instructions on how to make a grilled cheese."

"Hmmm," he murmurs. I feel his erection against my ass. He unsnaps my bra and lets his hands slide under my shirt until he is cupping my breast. "I love these." He manages to pull my bra through the shirtsleeves.

"You're being distracting." I bite my lip as he twists my nipples.

He backs away and I immediately feel bereft. "Finish our meal baby. I'm sorry. You're just so fucking sexy standing here in kitchen wearing my shirt." He slaps my ass and I yelp. He sure loves my ass.

We eat our meal and it is actually delicious. Grayson compliments my cooking and I beam with pride. I polish off two glasses of the merlot before he is leading me back to the bedroom. He actually waits patiently as I wrap up my homework even though he's so hard, he can break something—namely me. As soon as my textbook closes, he is on me with the quickness. He pulls the shirt off over my head and latches on to my nipple. He swirls his tongue around the peaks and I'm already squirming. He lays me down and rrriiippp. There go my panties. He snakes down between my legs and lifts my hips. He holds me snugly as he buries his face between my thighs. "Shit," I scream. He has me coming in record time, but he doesn't stop. He alternates his licks with nibbles and sucking to my nub. His rhythm has me on edge again. I can't reach his hair since he has my hips suspended mid-air, so I grip the sheets as my orgasm rolls over the first one. He brings me to one more orgasm before I feel him at my entrance.

"I'm going to fuck you now baby. I will not be gentle or slow. I'll make love to you later, but right now my dick is so hard for you. This will be pure unadulterated fucking." As promised, he plunges into me and I slide forward from the force. His punishing strokes have my legs trembling and my sex clinching as I take all that he is giving me.

I watch as his bicep muscles flex as he holds me in his strong embrace. Sweat beads down his face and chest as he works me over. He puts my legs over his shoulders to get deeper and holy hell. This new angle has me stretched to capacity. I grab his ass to push him further still. "Fuck," he screams as he continues his relentless stroke. I'm so glad Jordan's gone. "You're fucking milking my cock baby. So damn good." He grabs my hair and pulls as he finds his release. This is enough for me to come with him. We are both spent.

"That was incredible," he says while pulling me in to

cuddle.

"Yes," is the only comment I can muster.

"Sleep now love." We cuddle and everything is right in the world. I fall asleep content that I have a man that truly loves me.

SUNLIGHT FILTERS THROUGH my curtains, bringing with it a new day. Today is my long day, but I welcome it. It's funny how a little sex, okay a lot of sex, can give you a renewed sense of purpose. I can hear my shower going so I know that Grayson is still here. My alarm hasn't gone off yet so I know we have some playtime. I think I'll join him in the shower. My sore limbs and nether region protests this idea as I make a move to exit the bed. I smile at the memories of how I got this way.

My insatiable desires are crushed by Jordan's voice on the other side of the door.

"Liam, wait!" Too late. He opens my door and I quickly cover myself with the sheet.

"Get up lazy bones. I thought maybe we could grab a bite to eat and ride into school together," he says jokingly. Jordan and I exchange worried glances, but he misinterprets our concern. "Siobhan, I've seen every inch you. There's no need for modesty. Shower and get dressed so we can stop at that bakery you love so much." It is at his mention of a shower that he looks toward the bathroom. He hears the shower cut off and realizes that I'm not alone. His face ashen as he balls up his fists. Jordan grabs him by the hand in an effort to lead him out of my room, but he doesn't budge. "Liam, let's talk later. I can meet you in the cafeteria after my third class," I plead.

"Who is he?" His eyes are piercingly hard as he walks toward me. Just then Grayson steps out of the bathroom, clad in only a towel. *Holy hell. Shit just got real.* Droplets of water bead down his chest and he looks like a wet dream. Even Jordan does a double take. The initial confusion on his face indicates that he had been oblivious to the scene unfolding out here in the bedroom. He processes the situation instantly and growls at Liam's proximity to me. Especially while only a sheet separates my nudity.

"You're fucking our professor? You give me shit and you're banging the god damn professor?" He yanks on his hair as he backs away from me, shaking his head in disgust. "Is that how you earned that A you got in the class, by being his whore?" My jaw drops at the absurdness and venom that is spewing from his mouth. Grayson rushes him and pins him against the door. I squeal in fear that Grayson is going to beat the shit out of him.

"First off, she's no longer my student you little fucking punk. Don't be mad that you couldn't keep your infinitesimal dick in your pants and she moved on to someone better." Liam squirms against his grip, but his attempt is futile. "You call my girlfriend a whore and actually think I'm going to let you walk out of here? Apologize now motherfucker before I beat the snot out of you." Jordan is smiling from ear to ear at Liam's predicament. *Unbelievable.* Grayson's towel is hanging on by a thread now and I know I must step in and do something before his junk makes its debut to these two. I wrap the sheet tight around me and hobble my way to where the two men are posted against the door.

Liam is intent on being a tough guy. "Get the fuck off me. I will have your job, you predatory sick fuck." I slide my hand in between the two men and try to pry them apart.

chapter 8

GRAYSON IS TEMPORARILY distracted by my appearance in their scuffle. He glances down at my bootless leg and frowns. This momentary preoccupation that I'm bearing weight on my ankle allows Liam to aim for a sucker punch. I see his intent and try to stop him. *What the fuck was I thinking?* While Grayson is looking down, I step in the direct path of Liam's fist— thinking he would halt his attempt. I misjudged the quickness of his swing. A crushing blow lands on the side of my face and I'm falling. It all happens so fast. Jordan is screaming now and is at my side within seconds. Excruciating pain radiates through my jaw, causing tears to fall heavily. There is no saving Liam now. "I'm going to kill you motherfucker!" Grayson booms. He is all fists as he unleashes his fury at Liam. I'm still on the floor, but I plead with Jordan to stop Grayson. Liam is in a ball now taking the punishment Grayson is serving up. Jordan jumps on his back from behind in an effort to still his murderous hands and their assault.

"Please stop Grayson. You're scaring her. I know this ass wipe deserves a beat down, but your girl needs you more." I'm crying harder now because I don't want him to get in trouble over me. Surely Liam knows that I'm not a whore. He, of all people, knows that. He was speaking from hurt and anger. I know the feeling. I've been there. Grayson takes a moment to process Jordan's words before reluctantly getting off of Liam. He walks over to me and scoops me up before wiping my tears. "I'm sorry baby," he whispers, still breathing hard.

Anguish crosses his handsome face as he studies mine. I can feel the bruise starting to form. He glances Liam's way with contempt and I hug him tighter. I don't want him to go back and finish the job. Liam finally gains his footing. Sorrow is in the depth of his eyes as he visualizes me literally in the arms of another man.

"I'm so sorry Shiv," he says. He dejectedly walks out the door. The alarm on my phone picks this time to ring, signaling I should be getting ready for class. Jordan leaves now to give us privacy. Grayson caresses the lump forming along my jawline and flinches.

"Grayson, it's okay. I'll be alright," I say reassuringly.

"But it's not all right. That little cunt put his hands on you," he spits.

"It wasn't intentional. He was trying to take a swing at you. I know that he wouldn't purposefully hurt me."

"Are you defending him now?" He asks in shock. "If calling you a whore and accusing you of sleeping with me for a grade isn't purposefully being hurtful, I don't know what is."

He couldn't be more right. "You're right baby and no I'm not defending him. I just don't want you to get into trouble with the university. Truth is, I've never seen him behave this way and it's my fault. I hurt him and I don't know what he is going to do about it." Grayson sits us on the bed. He lifts my chin so that I'm looking him in the eyes.

"You don't owe him shit. You weren't his girl. I didn't steal you away. His lack of realization that he had a gem was his fault, not yours. You gave him a chance over what… five or six years? He blew it. It doesn't matter what my profession is. We're two people who were meant to find each other. He left the door open for me baby when he snuck out to play with the unworthy. And for that, I'm grateful." He kisses my bruise softly before finding my lips. The kiss is tender and nurturing, seeking confirmation that things between us are indeed okay. I return his kiss to show that we are more than okay.

"I have a class to teach baby, but are you still going in? Maybe you should rest for today."

"Nonsense. Nothing a little concealer won't fix. Besides, I have homework to turn in and quizzes to take," I smile.

"Okay, just take it easy. Can I see you tonight?" And just like that, his wicked perversion is back. The gleam in his eyes tells me where his thoughts have wandered.

"Sure, today is my long day though. Why don't you come over around seven or eight. I'll have Jordan cook us something truly gourmet other than my grilled cheese." He laughs at my offer.

"I'll call when I'm on the way. Don't go through any trouble on my account. I can eat whatever. Especially when you're going to be the dessert," he winks.

I SIT HERE in the cafeteria watching the other students interact. I've pushed my uneaten pizza aside, unable to eat. It's been two weeks since the incident with Liam and he has managed to avoid me like the plague. I don't like these unsettled feelings between us. I still care about him as a friend. Although, I don't feel as though I owe him an explanation about my relationship with Grayson, I can't stand how we left things. Grayson has been away on business for this past last week so I feel alone. I glance at the time and note that I have fifteen minutes before my last class. Since having my boot removed yesterday, I'm able to get around much quicker. I dump my uneaten pizza in the trash, grab my messenger bag, and head to my finance class.

Professor Gradney is busy writing today's objectives on the board as I take my seat with three minutes to spare. Little attention is given to my note taking. Instead I doodle Grayson's name and let my mind wander to what he could be doing at this moment. It must be quite a feat to divide his time between Michaels' Enterprises and teaching. His dedication to giving back through sharing his business knowledge makes him even hotter. I hold on to this piece of info in my quest to be unselfish when I'm missing him so much. Class ends and I'm determined to find a way to keep my mind busy.

I'm actually looking forward to margarita Monday. By the time I make it to our arranged meeting spot at the library, Jordan is already sitting on the stairs. She is talking away on her cell, so she doesn't notice my arrival. She nearly jumps out of her skin when I sit next to her.

"What the hell Shiv?" She places a hand on her chest in exasperation. "You can't sneak up on people like that."

"I didn't. You were so wrapped up in your conversation

you didn't see me. Who are you talking to anyway?" *As if I can't guess.* She and Trevor have been joined at the hip lately. I'm happy to see that she has someone special. And it doesn't hurt that she has been open minded about my relationship with Grayson.

"Whatever," she blushes. "Trevor, I'll call you tomorrow. Tonight is girl's night," she says ending her call. I tease her for a bit before we make plans to stop at the liquor store on the way home.

I SIP ON the last of my wine, allowing myself to succumb to my buzz. Life is good. I have a man that I adore, my stalker calls have been non-existent, and I'm in good company. I watch as Meghan and Bailey polish off the last two slices of the pizza and complain about the professors they hate taking this semester. My phone chirps, alerting me that I have an incoming text.

Grayson: What are you doing sexy?

Me: Who is this?

Grayson: Who do you want it to be love?

Inside, I'm doing a happy dance that he's contacted me. I decide to play this game a little longer.

Me: Hmmm. My lover. I miss his cock.

Grayson: Someone's been drinking.

```
Me: Maybe

Grayson:  It  wasn't  a  question
babe.  Margarita  Monday  right?
Why  don't  you  bring  your  sexy  ass
outside?  Your  lover  is  waiting  in
the  limo.
```

Damn, he knows me well.

I'm dressed in sweats and a tank, but if I change, I'll draw attention to me leaving. I make some lame excuse about asking a neighbor to join our booze fest and the girls buy it. Jordan knows better, but simply smiles in understanding. The cool air snips at my exposed arms. My flip-flop clad feet help to quicken my pace as I round the corner looking for the limo. The driver sees me approaching and wastes no time opening the door for me. Grayson frowns when he sees how I'm dressed.

"Where in the hell are your clothes? It's too cold for you to be dressed like it's god damn Summer time," he barks. I jump at his assertion. Dominance is one thing in the bedroom, but outside of sex, it catches me off guard. "Get in," he says lowering his voice some.

"Well, hello to you too. Welcome back." His eyes lose some of their hardness and he grabs my hands.

"Sorry for yelling sweetheart. I just don't want you getting sick trying to see me. That was not my intent. I just wanted to surprise you."

His concern is endearing. I want to diffuse any lingering unpleasant vibes. I reach up and bring his face to mine and he rewards me with a sensuous kiss. The remaining goose bumps that weren't dissipated from the heat circulating in the limo disappear the moment his hands touch me. He pulls me onto his lap and I straddle his muscular thighs. He palms my ass as he thrusts his erection upward. He sucks on my neck and I'm dizzy with desire.

"I've missed you so much baby." The sound of the privacy screen rising reminds me that we're not alone. I look in the direction of the driver's seat, but he is no longer visible. "He can't see or hear us love," Grayson says while removing my tank. One flick to the clasp in the front of my bra and my naked breasts are on display for him. The heat in his eyes is unmistakable. *Shit this is really happening.* I look around the parking lot and I can see people walking to their cars. I instinctively cover my breasts.

"Grayson, are you sure nobody can see us?" He removes my arms slowly and takes a nipple into his mouth. "Grrrrrayson," I whimper.

"I promise nobody can see us baby. Let me fuck you. I can't wait until this weekend. I miss you too much." He doesn't wait for me to respond. He continues his assault on my other nipple. It doesn't take long for wetness to pool between my legs.

He lays me down on the limo seat and pulls frantically at my sweats until they're in a pile on the limo floor with the rest of my clothes. "This is going to be quick baby." He reaches down to ensure that I'm wet enough. When he is satisfied that I am, he pulls down his own slacks and boxers to his knees. He positions himself at my entrance before he plunges in and holy hell.

"Oh Grayson," I moan. My verbalization spurs him on. He throws one of my legs over his shoulder and this new depth has me holding on to his shoulders to brace myself for the pounding he is giving me. He angles his hips in a delicious rhythm as he grinds even deeper.

"Fuck...so good baby," he growls. His punishing strokes are relentless. I grab his hair as he pushes me over the edge. I scream his name and a wicked smirks forms on his lips. "Mine," he claims as he finds his own release inside me. He falls forward to lay on top me. His chest heaves as he works to catch his breath.

"Damn, I needed that," I confess, courtesy of the wine. I play with his hair and kiss the side of his face. He flips us over and now I'm resting on top of him.

"I needed that more than you did. I've thought about you nonstop all week." We did talk on the phone, but between his meetings and my classes, it wasn't often enough. We talked briefly before turning in each night, but that just made me miss him even more.

Our post-coital haze is interrupted by a pull of the handles on the limo door. *What the hell?* "Grayson are you in there?" Bailey's inquisitive voice penetrates through the door and I'm scrambling to put my clothes back on. The limo driver gets out and tries to diffuse the situation.

"How does she know that this is your limo Grayson?" I whisper hiss.

"It has to be the license plate. It's a custom plate babe. Sorry, I didn't think about that. I just came here straight from the airport because I needed to see you." He pulls up his pants, but his shirt is still unbuttoned and his hair has that just fucked look I love so much.

"Oh. My. God. Please don't let her in. I didn't tell her that I was seeing you. Does she know?"

"Unfortunately not love. She hasn't seen our parents lately because they're in Europe for a convention. As far as Vanessa, I made her promise not to spill the beans— I thought it would be better coming from me. I just haven't had the opportunity to talk to her because of this business trip. I don't want her to find out I'm seeing her brother like this. We can hear her arguing with the driver.

"I know he's in there, Stanley. I could hear moving around in there when I first walked up. Look, I already sent my only ride away rather than have her drive out of her way to take me home. I don't give a shit who he has in there. I need a ride home." Her frustration is evident.

"I have to let her in sweetheart. I can't have my sister freezing her ass off out there and stranded without a ride. We can do this. It's only a matter of time before our parents deliver the news anyway. We can tell her together." He looks at me for reassurance and I nod.

He opens the limo door and I couldn't have been prepared for Bailey's reaction if I tried. She just stands there, slack mouthed, in shock. It takes a moment for her to process my presence. "What the fuck is going on? You're screwing my brother?" Damn. Grayson didn't even bother fixing his shirt, although I'm sure it doesn't take a genius to guess what we've been up to. I have no words.

"Bailey. We didn't want you to find out like this, but Siobhan and I are dating." He reaches for her, but she steps back.

"How long has this been going on? Fuck. This is why Vanessa has been an emotional mess. Shiv is the reason why you cut your friendship off with her," she accuses.

"Siobhan and I started seeing each other casually last semester and it's blossomed into something more. My relationship with Vanessa is complicated," he attempts to explain. Bailey turns her glare towards me. "You've befriended me, yet you sleep with my brother behind my back. I trusted you and you've been a lying bitch this whole time."

Her words hurt because I know I should've shared that trust she extended and told her sooner.

"I'm sorry Bailey. I should have—" She cuts me off with a wave of her hand. Grayson tries to stop her ranting, but she talks over him.

"I don't want your fucking apology. Day late...dollar short. I no longer trust you. An omission is still a lie. You had a whole semester to come clean. He's never acknowledged you. How does that make you feel to know you were his dirty little secret?"

chapter
9

"BAILEY, SHUT THE hell up. You don't have all the information." He is arguing with her, but I take this moment to sprint back towards the condo. This is the second time I've been accused of being a whore. Bailey may not have stated those exact words, but they were implied. I'm just fucking up friendships left and right. I can't face Jordan right now. Instead of heading back to our unit, I head towards the pool. The gates are locked so I take a seat on the ground and lean against them. I let the tears fall freely now for the chaos that is my life. All facets of my life can never line the hell up. As soon as one aspect is going well, something else plunges me pack into misery.

I smell his expensive cologne without looking up. "Get up baby. You're going to get sick out here." I look up at him and he grimaces at my tear-stained face. He pulls me up and kisses my eyelids. "Our road won't be an easy one sweetheart, especially because of the way we started, but you're worth it for me. Bailey was out of line. I'll talk to her once she gets over the initial shock and calms down. For now, I had Stanley take her home. Now come on, let's get you inside." He takes his suit jacket off and wraps it around me. I'm hurting so I smart off, "Yeah, let's get your dirty little secret inside before someone sees you."

He steps closer to me until my back is against the gate. "Don't you dare fucking do that. You already know how I feel about you. Don't ever let someone else's words or misconceptions make you doubt the love I have for you. I'm not good at expressing my feelings so I need you to believe in us." He grabs my hand and starts pulling me along. "I'm taking your ass inside. I need to fuck you into a good mood again. You need my attitude adjuster."

"Your attitude adjuster?" I struggle to keep pace with his brisk walking.

"My cock love. It's your personal attitude adjuster," he smirks.

"Oh. My. God. You are so crass. Your cock is not a fix all smart ass." I can't help but smile. His serious intent on making me feel better with his penis is so out there, it's funny. He has a way of making everything fade in the background except me and him. I can't stay upset around him. He won't let me. His cocky ways are endearing and infectious.

"So you say babe, but the mere mention of my cock, and those tears are gone." He winks at me and I slap his arm. Crap, he's right. "You're even smiling. In a few minutes you'll be screaming out in pleasure. If that is not an attitude adjuster, I don't know what is."

We enter the condo laughing, but Jordan is in the living room pacing. "Shiv, are you okay? Bailey called me upset. She shared with me the lashing she gave you." Grayson pinches the bridge of his nose in frustration. He doesn't want me to slide back into my somber mood.

"Let's talk later, okay?" I give her a hug to reassure her that I'm okay. *For now.*

"Thank fuck," Grayson exclaims.

The minute we enter my room I'm surprised by Grayson's actions. He takes out his phone and scroll through it for a few seconds before placing it on my iHome docking station on my nightstand. Lifehouse's "Everything" begins to play from the speakers and I'm so moved. I can't help the tears that fall, but these are happy tears. He knows how much music means to me. He said he has a difficult time expressing himself so he is using the music as a form of expression. He saunters over to where I'm still standing by the door.

"Listen to the lyrics baby. They convey my love for you so perfectly." He uses his thumb to wipe away my tears before placing a chaste kiss to my lips. He eases me down to the chair I have in the corner and places my feet on the ottoman. "Sit here. I'm going to run us a bath. Have you eaten?" I simply nod because I'm still in shock at his tender side. Satisfied with my answer, he walks to my bathroom and closes the door. I can hear the bath water running. What had escalated to a shitty day is now looking up. Grayson doesn't see that the attitude adjuster is him. His cock is just an added bonus. I'm so irrevocably in love with this man. He has managed to not just alter my mood, but my perception and receptiveness to love as well. I'm now willing to let go and let love in.

I'm pulled out of my reverie by the sound of the bathroom door opening. Grayson strides past me and out of my room. He briefly converses with Jordan before returning to the room with two wine glasses and a bottle of pinot grigio.

He doesn't say a word to me, he just grabs the iHome and takes it all to the bathroom. I don't have to wait long, he is at my side in seconds pulling me up. "Come love." *Wow.* The lavender aroma permeating from the bath is heavenly. Little tea lights are placed along the tub and help to create a romantic ambiance. He shuffles through the music on his phone until he finds the playlist he's looking for. Joi's *Lick* starts to play and I giggle. So gone is the lovey-dovey music. He has replaced it with music that conveys he wants to fuck. I gather that my assessment is correct from the sudden wickedness in his eyes. He slowly unbuttons his dress shirt and I'm spellbound. His chest and abs are a picture of perfection. Every etched line screams to be licked. He sees the lust in my eyes and begins to remove his pants just as slowly. The massive bulge in front of his boxer briefs is unmistakable.

He walks over to me and lifts my tank over my head before licking the swells of my breasts pushed up by my demi-cup bra. "I love these," he murmurs. He unsnaps the front clasp and my double D breasts falls heavily against my chest.

He cups them in his palms and massages them. "I want my dick right here," he smiles. He yanks off my sweats and panties as one. His eyes peruse my body, yet I'm surprisingly at ease with my nudity. "Damn, your body is so amazing love." He spins me around and grabs my ass. "This ass is my favorite." I can tell that he has removed his briefs because his naked erection is nudging my ass. He tilts my head to the side so that he can place tender kisses along my neck. One hand splays across my stomach while the other hand fists my hair. A small moan slips past my lips as I melt into him.

"Hmmm, I think you like it a little rough. I like the way your body responds to the hair pulling. I plan to find out what else your body likes." He gives my hair a slight tug to test his theory and I nearly come undone. I grind my ass against his erection, desperate to soothe this ache he is causing between my legs.

"Please Grayson." My voice cracks as I struggle to maintain control. He smiles knowingly and guides me to the tub.

"Patience love." He gets into the bath first before assisting me to take a seat between his legs. "Let me take care of you." He pours us a glass of wine before leaning us back against the tub. His hand in my hair is gentle now as he massages my scalp.

We listen to slow romantic music by various artists and continue to finish off the entire bottle of wine. I'm relaxed and horny as hell. The wine has heightened my libido and is driving my boldness. I want this sex god now. No more swooning. I turn to face him and inch forward until I'm straddling his thighs. I rub myself against his hardness while I capture his lips in a searing kiss. He is caught off guard by my forwardness for a second, but then he returns my enthusiasm. His tongue duels mine in a punishing kiss. In my continuance of taking the lead, I grab his cock and place it at my entrance. I slide down, taking each delicious inch until I've taken all of him. "Grayson," I moan.

"That's right baby. Take what you want from me." He grips my hips and I begin to move. His girth stretches me wide as my slow grind already threatens to push me over the edge. I can feel Grayson's corded thigh muscles tighten beneath me as we begin to pick up the tempo. And just like that, my lead is taken away. He sets an Olympic pace as he impales me on his cock faster and so much harder. Gone is the tenderness. The man in front of me is raw and unapologetic with his fucking. "Damn, your pussy is so good baby. Fuck, I can't get deep enough." He angles his hips and I damn near feel his length in my stomach. Water sloshes over the side of the tub as the rhythm picks up even more.

I'm sure Jordan is getting our sexcapade in surround sound, but I can't bring myself to care. Grayson yanks my hair back, exposing my neck to him. His teeth sink into my skin and it is enough to send us both over the edge. I scream out his name, extending the syllables as I ride out my orgasm.

"Damn, I love how vocal you've become love. I bet the neighbors know my name with that pronouncement. So fucking hot!" I flush crimson. I may as well have given Jordan front row tickets to the show. I cover my face, but Grayson is not having it. "Don't be ashamed of your sexuality. Own it. Embrace it." His erection rises above the water line between us and I smile. Seems like I'm not the only insatiable one.

"Well that was fast," I say looking down at his cock.

"It's you sweetheart. I just can't get enough. Come on, let's get out. I want you in the bed." When we get into the bedroom, Grayson picks me up and throws me on the bed. Sexual deviance stares back at me as he stealthily climbs into the bed. He grabs me by the ankles and pulls me the rest of the way to him. My body hums from his dominance. He wraps my legs around his waist and I tingle with anticipation. He leans down and kiss me ever so gently, but I don't want gentle. I want to scream. *Take me damn it.*

His right hand slides down to the base of my neck and a small gasp slips past my lips. My back arches on its own accord as I grip the sheets. Grayson smiles wickedly as he tightens his grip. He watches closely for my reaction so I can't hide my desire to have him squeeze tighter. Moisture pools between my legs and I begin to claw at his arms. I need more. This is a side of me that I'm not familiar with. He loosens his hold and I can't help the disappointment that ensues. "Interesting," he says. He plunges his shaft in me and I grip his ass so that he'll go deeper. He wanted me sexually uninhibited, well here I am.

"Please don't stop," I beg.

"Not a chance love." His hands find my throat again and I begin to tremble with need.

"Please Grayson. Do it." I don't have to explain what 'it' is.

"I need you to tap my arms if it gets to be too much baby." I nod my understanding, but this is unsatisfactory. "No. I need you to verbalize that you understand," he insists.

"I understand. I will tap your arms if your hold is too much," I assure. The predatory gleam in his eyes is back as his smile broadens. His grip tightens on my neck as he fucks me with fervor. He alternates the intensity of his hold around my neck with each stroke. The feeling is intense.

The initial sensation of oxygen loss brings about an uncertainty. Before I can panic though, Grayson slightly releases his hold again and holy hell. Stars begin to dance behind my closed eyes as the feeling of falling takes over. He continues this erotic strangulation sequence as he pounds me into oblivion. I can feel the build-up and I've never felt this orgasmic. I'm completely euphoric when my orgasm ripples through me. Grayson finds his own release and we ride out the waves together. I don't know what the fuck that was and the aftermath scares me. I can't believe I asked him to choke me. Who is this person I'm becoming? I'm so ashamed. When he pulls out, I turn on my side to face away from him.

"That was fucking earth shattering love." He forces me to turn to face him. "Don't hide from me. You're discovering your sexuality, that's all. You're learning what turns you on. If you enjoy breath play, that's okay. I'll make sure you're safe."

"What the hell is breath play? How can I like something if I don't know what it is?"

"Breath play is what we were doing. It is also called erotic asphyxiation. Basically a fancy term for purposefully withholding oxygen to the brain for sexual arousal. It can be quite dangerous if not practiced right. You naturally gravitated toward this type of play from the mere touch of my hands to your neck and that's perfectly okay." He strokes away the hair that is drenched in sweat and sticking to my face.

"Ha. You didn't say perfectly normal. You think I'm nuts. Who the hell in their right mind asks to be choked?" I went from being sexually inexperienced to sexually dark in the blink of a relationship.

"To hell with normal babe. We're creating our own normal and that is all that matters. I love that you trust me enough to allow yourself to be sexually free. I won't let you fall. Ever." His promise to protect me warms my heart while simultaneously frightening me that he has experience with such an act.

"Grayson? How is it that you're so comfortable with breath play?" The smile drops from his face in an instant. He momentarily looks away before facing me again. He studies my reaction as he carefully chooses his words.

"Siobhan, my sexual history is extensive—some I'm not proud off. I've experimented with the many facets of sex and have very distinguished taste. My sexual appetite is pronounced and my stamina can be intimidating. This is my past and part of our future. My past sexual encounters have no bearing on our relationship as I'm clean and always tested regularly. I do want to introduce you to my predilection of sex, but I will take it slow. You're on your own journey right now." His admittance of his extensive sexual history slightly disturbs me, but it is just that— *history*. This fact doesn't stop me from digging deeper though.

"Is this why you're considered a sex addict by your therapist?" He sits up and pulls me into his lap.

chapter 10

"I'M NOT YOUR textbook sex addict nor am I what you may visualize. My libido doesn't affect my job, I'm not harboring a huge selection of porn, and sex doesn't consume my every waking thought. My sexual desires are not compulsive or uncontrolled. My hypersexuality and the emotional suppression that was attached to the stigma of sex earned me the classification. There are varying degrees to sex addiction, but it is an addiction no less." His uneasiness is transparent. He is worried I may run. "I love hard, Siobhan. There is no threat that I will cheat on you. I can't promise not to corrupt or introduce you to my kinky ways though," he winks. He attempts to lighten a touchy subject, but his sincerity touches me. It is in this moment that I know that I will gladly step over to the debauchery side of sex with this man.

"Let me in Grayson. I want to know that side of you. I want all of you." I am pinned to the spot by his cerulean iridescence.

"Be sure you're ready for what you're asking love," he warns.

"I'm sure. I've never been more sure of anything before." He begins to kiss me slowly and I know the conversation is over. He flips over to lie on his back while positioning me to straddle him. I gladly insert his hardness inside me and start a leisurely grind. He brings us both to one last orgasm before we both fall asleep from exhaustion.

I'M STARTLED AWAKE by Jordan's presence at the end of my bed. "Get up my newly nympho friend," she giggles. "You guys made me listen to your marathon sex last night. Holy shit, that guy has stamina. I was slightly jealous that Trevor was out of town visiting his brother. Your woman bits should be beyond sore after that production." I look around, but his side of the bed is empty. The coolness of the sheets indicates he has been gone for some time.

"Jordan," I groan. I don't want to talk about my night of hot sex with Grayson, although she is right. My sex is really sore.

"What? I never heard Liam put it down like that. That man had you screaming his name. That was so fucking hot. All I could image is him in that damn towel and the water droplets beading down his eight pack. Shit, you're lucky. I may have been inclined to forgive him too."

"Oh. My. God. You're insufferable. Check out your own man," I laugh.

"Hey, I can't help it if I have eyes and ears. By the way, he left about two hours ago. He said he would call you later. He didn't want to wake you after your late night."

"He didn't say that last part, crazy ass," I chortle.

"No, but it was inferred. You guys were at it until at least one this morning."

"I can't believe you stayed up and clocked our sex time," I say shaking my head.

"Like I had a choice," she huffs. "On a serious note, Bailey is really pissed that you didn't tell her you were seeing her brother. She was upset with me too for a second, but then she realized it wasn't my news to share."

"Yeah, she kind of went bat shit crazy in the parking lot." I flinch at the recall.

"Well, I've arranged for us to have a girls' night this Friday at Drai's to squash this drama. I can't have my friend and my bestie on the outs with one another." Jordan places a hand on her hip, something that she unconsciously does when she is serious.

"I don't have an issue with her. I want to fix things. She's the one defending his relationship with Vanessa."

"We will get to the bottom of this Friday then," she insists. I hate agreeing without knowing if Grayson has plans for us this weekend, but this is important. I can't let things remain the way are between us.

"Okay, fine."

"Things will be back to normal by margarita Monday," Jordan assures. I'm not so sure. She leaves my room and I force myself up to get ready. My limbs scream in protest. I'm deliciously sore all over. I will indeed reminisce about last night with every step today. When I come out of the room, Jordan is in her usual spot sipping on her undoubtedly second or third cup of coffee. It makes me happy to resume our normal morning routine.

THE WEEK PAST blazingly fast. Grayson left on another business trip mid-week and won't be back until tomorrow so this little girls' night tonight worked out. Once again, my bed looks like my closet and dresser vomited clothes as I try to find something to wear. I hate trying to put a look together. I suck at it. Jordan stands in the doorway snickering at my frustration. She dangles a sequin dress on her finger. "I have a dress for you Shiv. I guess I should have told you before you wrecked your room," she chides. I march over to her and grab the dress, ready to be done with this hunt for an outfit. I rid myself of my tank and sweats and slide the taupe mini dress over my curves. It has a V-neckline, but it supports the girls. My ass on the other hand is a different story. The length hits me mid-thigh and I know from experience that any ass shaking will inch this baby right on up. Well, I don't plan on dancing much anyway. I will people watch tonight and try to resolve my issues with Bailey.

"This one will do."

"Are you freaking kidding me? You look hot!" She runs to her room and comes back with matching pumps. I haven't attempted to wear heels since I broke my ankle. I hope I don't bust my ass.

"We'll see if you're still saying that when you are picking me up off the floor. It's been a long time since I've worn heels."

"Pssh, whatever. It's like riding a bike. You'll be fine." She leaves me alone to do my own hair and make-up while she gets herself ready. When she comes back, my jaw nearly drops to the floor. Her dress is smoking and a bit risqué. It is black sequin with an open back. It barely covers her ass. I would be falling out of the bottom if she gave me that one to wear, but it is sexy as hell on her. "What do you think?" she says twirling in a circle.

"I think you're going to be fighting the men off with a stick without Trevor by your side tonight."

"We as in plural darling, but that's okay. We can hold our own. We can be the sexy sequin twins that you get to look at, but can't touch," she surmises.

"You can be such a dork, you know that right?"

"Yep and you wouldn't have me any other way." She laughs and I join her because she's right.

THE BASE OF the music vibrates through the floor. Bodies gyrate to the beat and completely fill the dance floor. The strobe lights and smog make it difficult to see what little path there is to make our way toward the pool bar. We finally make it to our reserved cabana and I stop short at the presence before me. Vanessa is sitting there, legs crossed in a body hugging dress of her own. *What the fuck is Bailey playing at?* I can't believe that she invited her.

My emotions are running high right now. I'm so pissed. I feel like I've been ambushed. Jordan grabs my hand and squeeze. "Did you fucking know that she was going to be here?"

"Of course not," she says affronted. "You know I wouldn't do that to you." It is at this moment that Meghan, Angie, and Bailey arrive carrying a hand full of drinks.

Bailey sees me and I just want to wipe the smirk off her face. "I see you girls have made it. I took the liberty of getting us started with tequila shots. Oh, and I invited Vanessa because I think if we are going to get to the bottom of this, she needs to be here." Jordan snarls and I can tell she is just as pissed as I am. "Please sit ladies."

I lead the way. I refuse to give them the satisfaction of having me walk out. Jordan follows suit. The other girls are clearly lost at the scene unfolding in front of them. I knock a couple shots back in rapid succession as I stare at the two of them sitting across from me.

"Okay, well I'll start us off. You ladies may not be aware, but Siobhan has been seeing my brother since last semester behind my back. She's had plenty of opportunities to be open with me, but instead she chose to sneak around with him," Bailey accuses. The girls look shocked at the news.

"Wait, I thought he was dating you Vanessa," Angie says.

"We were fucking, yes. Dating, no. Grayson and I were best friends. We always hooked up between his temps. Still our relationship was special." The girls turn to me for my explanation.

"Oh, cut the shit Vanessa. I didn't steal him from you. Look Bailey, I'm sorry I kept our relationship from you, but this is the very reaction I was trying to avoid. You all want the fucking sordid details, well here they are." Jordan shakes her head to let me know I don't have to tell them jack shit, but I'm fed up. They're all sitting here judging me while Vanessa sits back and plays the victim. "Grayson and I met because I was his student. The attraction was both mutual and instant. When Liam cheated on me, I just wanted the hurt to stop so I indulged in this attraction. On Bailey's birthday, we danced and that unleashed our hidden desires," I explain.

"He came to my party with Meredith. Jesus, you pulled him from her too?" Bailey interrupts.

"Don't be such a bitch Bailey," Jordan sneers. "You fucking wanted us here to try and see if you guys could hash things out. Stop with the ambush or we're leaving. *And that is why I love my bestie.* Bailey is shocked, but she shuts the hell up.

"After Meredith left to catch her plane, he came over that night. He said nothing happened between them and that he couldn't stay away from me. He left that night, but we agreed that I would call him the next day. From there we decided to enter into a casual, but exclusive relationship," I continue.

"Fuck buddies," Vanessa offers.

"Yes Vanessa, you could call it that. We couldn't be seen together since he was still my professor." I didn't want to share that bit of info even though I'm no longer his student, but Bailey left me no choice. "Initially, I didn't tell anyone because I couldn't. After I got to know you girls, I didn't want to share because honestly I knew he wasn't mine. It was only sex. Well, that's how it started off. I couldn't help the feelings that manifested along the way. He told me that he and Vanessa were close, but he wasn't seeing her. I was very aware that she hooked up with him between their 'temps,' as she put it. So you see, I didn't steal him. In jest, I started a sexual relationship; my very single professor, who I in turn, fell in love with." Bailey crosses her arms against her chest. She then closes her eyes and shakes her head— gathering her composure.

"You could have been honest with me, Siobhan. The way you went about it was wrong. To make matters worse, you made him choose between you and a friend that has been there for him when he didn't have his shit together. Vanessa was there when his engagement fell through. Did you know that? Did you know that he was once engaged?" Bailey inquires.

"Yes, he told me about Celeste," I spew. Vanessa cuts her off and I wonder what they're hiding. Why is the whole Celeste conversation so taboo? "I didn't make him stop being friends with Vanessa. The bullshit she pulled at the hospital put their friendship on the rocks. You didn't share that bit information, did you Vanessa?"

The horror stricken look on her face tells me that I've hit the nail on the head. The girls look at her for an explanation. "What is she talking about Vanessa?" Bailey asks.

"That was a private moment between us. I did realize that you were eavesdropping," she huffs, dodging Bailey's question. I plunge ahead.

"You allow everyone to paint you as the victim, but you fail to tell them that you came to harass me in the hospital when I couldn't get away." I turn toward the girls. "She warned me off Grayson and told me in so many words, how I meant nothing to him and that they had an unbreakable bond. She told me he was a sex addict that was using me to manipulate his therapy and how she was basically bidding her time until he was ready to be in a relationship again." I'm ready to spill it all. My trusty truth serum, Patron, has kicked in and I'm in the I-don't-give-a-fuck-mode. The girls gasp, but Bailey is shockingly silent. "Wait here is the best part. Grayson shows up and catches her leaving my room. She absolutely forbids him to see me, threatening exposure of our relationship if he took another step. He was pissed that she had crossed the line, but didn't want to call her bluff so he left. He told her then that their friendship was over. So you see, I didn't lay down that ultimatum, she did. It was either he left without seeing me or face exposure."

Vanessa stalks over toward me so I stand up. This in turn causes Jordan to stand up and an echo effect among the girls. She gets right in my face, undoubtedly embarrassed about being outed. "Fuck you Siobhan. He doesn't love you. He loves the idea of you. You're nothing more than a god damn stand in and you don't even know it," she rants. Bailey tugs at her arm to silence her, but it is too late. Inhibitions released, my hand flies and makes contact with her face. *Damn that felt good.*

"You bitch," she screams. She lurches forward, but I grab her hair and yank as hard as I can. She stumbles in her ridiculously high heels and knocks all the drinks off the table on her way down. *Stay down bitch.* Jordan and Angie pull me away while Bailey and Meghan help her up. The bouncers are at our table in seconds, but we assure them that we're leaving. Vanessa is sporting a cut lip from the fall and my drunken spirit grins at the payback. I'm pumped up now. Jordan helps to hold me up as we exit the club so I don't meet the same fate with the floor.

"Come on Muhammad Ali," she jokes. Huh, I just slapped her. I should have punched her sorry ass. How dare she get in my face? I wasn't in a hospital bed broken this time. She should've known that smart shit wouldn't fly twice. It's been a long time coming.

chapter 11

THE CRASHING OF pots and pans interrupts my plans to sleep through this hangover. I'm going to kill Jordan. She better be making my favorite crepes for the racket she's making, ugh. I listen closer and I realize she is going on and on about last night's events. God she must be telling Trevor about my finest moment. I can't say I regret it, although I hate altercations. A sexy, raspy voice answers her and I nearly trip over my comforter trying to get out of the bed. Grayson's here. My head throbs in protest at the sudden moment. I rub my temples and squint at the door. I need to get out there and shut Jordan up. My door swings open and my very own heartthrob is standing there looking like the Adonis he is. He looks yummy in his jeans and black fitted tee. He runs a hand through his disheveled hair and all I can think about is how I want to do that. "So, I heard I missed the showdown last night," he grins.

"Jordan," I groan.

"What?" She asks innocently standing behind him.

"He had already heard about it, I just filled him in on some of the details," she says sheepishly.

"Yeah, Vanessa called me crying about it last night and Bailey called me this morning."

"She had it coming Grayson. I—" he cuts me off.

"It's okay baby. I'm not mad. Come here." He reaches for me and pulls me into a hug. I wince from the headache. This doesn't escape his attention. "Let's sit you on the bed so we can work on getting rid of this hangover." He asks Jordan to point him in the direction of where we keep the aspirin. He comes back with medicine and orange juice in hand. "Take this and lay down while I fix you some breakfast. Jordan made vegetable omelets." True to his word, he is back within minutes with a tray of piping hot coffee and an omelet. Jordan walks in and heads to my closet. I watch as she pulls out my carry-on luggage bag and begins to rummage through my dresser for clothes.

"What are you doing?"

"Ask your man," she smiles. She continues on her quest of packing for me, but why?

"Grayson, what's going on?"

"I'm taking you on a little overnight trip," he winks. "Remember what we talked about last time I was here." We talked about a lot of stuff. He is going have to be a little more specific, but somehow I'm guessing that is the point.

"Enlighten me, old sneaky one," I deadpan. He throws his head back and out comes the sexiest laugh I've ever heard.

"Your sarcasm is so endearing love." He leans down and kisses me on the head, careful not to cause me pain.

"Shiv, where is your passport?" That gets my attention. *What the hell?* "Never mind, found it," she says looking in the shoebox I keep in the top of my closet. My curiosity has definitely been stroked.

"Grayson, are you seriously not going to tell me where we're going?" He had my apt attention at Jordan's mention of passport. I hate flying. I know I have better odds of being in a car crash, yada yada, yada. But seeing as though, I've already done the car crash thing, I think my odds of being in a plane crash have increased. Irrational fear, I think not. Now that the coffee and aspirin have helped to ease my headache, I get up to see what Jordan has picked out for me. She informs me that we will discuss last night's events when I get back. *Oh yay!!!* While Grayson is busy bringing my things to his car, I use this time to shower and brush my teeth. I don't have time to dry my hair so I wrap it in a bun. I struggle with pulling my jeans on with the dampness of my skin and my ass that should have its own zip code.

"You need some help with that love?" I startle at Grayson's presence in the doorway. He saunters over and caresses my ass before slapping it. "What are you trying to do to me?"

"You're getting yourself riled up. Help me with my jeans perv," I joke. He slides my jeans over my ass with one deft pull. The heat from his fingers causes a tingle down below, but I do my best to ignore it. Starting something now will ensure that we don't make it to our intended destination. I put on a red cable knit sweater and ankle boots and I'm ready as I ever will be for this flight to God knows where.

We enter Grayson's private jet and I'm not surprised by its opulence. Leather recliners line the path on either side with wood grain trimmings and plush carpeting throughout. I take in very little of it in though, as my nerves begin to get the best of me. Grayson's perceptiveness has him ordering us a glass of wine from the flight attendant.

"I'm going to need something stronger," I say taking a seat in one of the recliners.

"You have me," he winks. *How cute.* He doesn't understand my fear of flying, but he will. He takes a seat next to me and places a soft kiss to my temple. He buckles us both in and I pout.

"I want you lucid, not inebriated because once we reach our cruising altitude I going to induct you into the mile-high club," he teases. Leave it to my sex-crazed boyfriend to use this as an opportunity to have sex. Who am I to argue? The pilot comes on over the intercom to announce our departure. He gives generalized information regarding our flight duration, weather conditions, and our anticipated arrival time. He leaves out the actual destination, courtesy of Grayson, I'm sure. The plane begins taxing down the tarmac and I turn to grab Grayson's arm. Wait, where is my wine?

"Grayson, the flight attendant didn't bring my wine."

"I know love. We were running late so we missed our chance to unwind before take-off. She's buckled in now. We'll get you a drink as soon as the seat belt light turns off."

"I needed it now," I murmur. I bury my head in his chest as we take flight. He strokes my hair and it's soothing me somewhat. Before I know it, the pilot is announcing that we are free to move about the cabin. Grayson clicks open my seat belt and pulls me into his lap. "Oh baby, come here." He pulls my bun free from its elastic and my red tresses tumble down past my breasts. "I've been meaning to do that. I told you, I like it down. You hair is so beautiful," he smiles. He signals for the flight attendant and she promptly brings our drinks. I feel myself relaxing into him more as the wine starts to do its job. He quirks a knowing eyebrow at me. He stands up, pulling me up with him. He guides us to the back of the plane and I know it's time for my induction.

We walk into the private bedroom and I'm speechless. It is gorgeous. The platform bed is obviously the feature piece. A mahogany headboard with several built-ins, acts as a divider for the room. The dim recessed lighting lends a romantic vibe along with the fireplace on the opposite side of the room. Damn, this is his life. I'm so out of my league.

"What are you thinking about?" he says from behind me.

"All of this," I say while motioning toward all this luxury surrounding us.

"It's just things love. You are what matters." I turn to face him to give a smart-ass remark, but the hunger in his eyes has me distracted. "I need your clothes off, now!"

He lifts me up and I wrap my legs around his waist. Using one hand, he pulls my sweater over my head. His fingers trace a trail between my breasts until he reaches the clasp at the front of my bra. "Best fucking invention ever," he swears. He springs them free and immediately takes a nipple into his mouth. He walks us over to the bed and lays me down. He rids himself of his clothes and I watch like it's my very own striptease. Every line etched in his muscled body acts to prime me. I just want to lick him. He winks when he catches me ogling him. "Like what you see?"

"Yes," I say boldly. I start undoing my own pants, but he stops me.

"Let me," he insists. He pulls my jeans and panties off so I'm completely naked. "Jesus, you're beautiful." He crawls onto the bed and puts my legs over his shoulders. His tongue parts me and I bite my lip to keep from squealing. He makes a twirling motion to my clit that drives me insane. I look down at him and he is watching intensely just how wild he is driving me. It is so fucking sexy. I grab his hair and ride his face. He is nibbling and licking and I can't hold back the scream that rips from me as my orgasm hits. He continues his tongue acrobatics, lapping my juices with enthusiasm. A wicked smile forms on his gorgeous face as my legs begin to tremble.

"Hmmm, that's what I was waiting for. I want you vocal baby. Don't hold it in." Shit, I just let the entire flight crew know that we're in here fucking. They probably guessed as much, but still. Maybe the room is sound proof. "Get out of your head sweetheart. I know what you're thinking. The fact that we're no longer out there, tells the crew what we're in here doing. I'm determined to get you over that sexual shyness of yours."

"You did that on purpose. You made me forget where I was. You and your wicked orgasms." He chuckles at my assessment.

"Now may be the time to share something with you love," he says cryptically.

"Okay." What the heck is he going to tell me?

"You remember you wanted me to let you in? You wanted all of me, including my brand of kink," he says reminding me of our conversation.

"I remember and I do." He kisses me and I taste myself on his tongue.

"I'm an exhibitionist love. I like to be watched. I want the person watching to see my lover in the throes of passion, as I bring her orgasm after orgasm. The more vocal you are, the harder I get. That is why I don't get off watching porn. I'm not a voyeur. I'm a hands on, watch me bring her to her knees, kinky motherfucker." Holy shit. *What the hell have I just asked for?*

"Shit, I don't know what to say. That is so out of my comfort zone. You let people watch you have sex?" He smiles as he tucks a strand of hair behind my ear.

"Not how you think. I don't just pull my dick out in public and fuck. It's been a while since I've indulged in this fantasy. I've suppressed this aspect of myself because I didn't want to just experience this with anyone." He's said a mouth full and I don't know how to process it all.

"So when was the last time you uh, did this in public?" I don't know if I want him to really answer that. Is this what he did with Vanessa? Is this something I could ever give him?

"I don't make it a practice to fuck in public sweetheart. I've done it, but it was more of an adrenaline rush of not getting caught. When I indulge in exhibitionism, I fuck freely and openly. This is done in a club setting."

"Oh. My. God. On the dance floor? Where?" I'm a glutton for punishment. He chuckles as my naivety.

"Not a regular club. A sex club with like-minded individuals." *Oh my.* "We're heading to Puerto Morelos, Mexico baby. I have a club there where select VIP members get to act out their fantasies. I want to bring you over to my world. I haven't shared this side of myself with anyone since Celeste," he explains. This is a lot to consider. I don't know if I can. Shit, this is the beyond the sixty he warned me about.

"Grayson…I—," he cuts me off.

"Shhh, it's okay love. There's no pressure. I will take you to the club tonight, but we won't do anything you're not ready for. And if you're never ready, that's okay too," he reassures.

Although, I hate hearing that he shared this with Celeste, she is his past and I'm his future. *Hopefully.* This is the first time I've allowed myself to visualize a future with him. It makes my heart happy that he hasn't shared this piece of himself with Vanessa. I want to share this with him, I just hope that I can. Grayson's light kisses to my neck pull me out of my reverie. He is a master at pulling me into the moment with him. My trepidation is forgotten as the ache down below makes itself known. He throws my leg over his hip before he plunges in. Damn, he feels so good. Little whimpers escape my lips as I do my best to silence my pleasure. Grayson grabs my hair and gives it a small yank. He's already figured it out that I like it rough.

"Uh-Uh baby, give to me. Let me fucking hear you," he says as he fiercely pounds me. He must be able to hear how wet I am with every stroke. "You're so wet."

"Ahhhh," I yell intelligibly as he angles his hips.

"Fuck yeah, that's what I want." My screams bring out the beast him. Wet sounds and skin slapping echo throughout the room as he pushes me over the edge. One last thrust and he is going over with me. "Shit, that was hot. You're a natural screamer love. You just don't know it yet. You've suppressed this side of yourself too long, but I'm going to unleash her," he smiles wickedly.

I'm so spent. Grayson cuddles up behind me and we fall asleep. Two hours pass before we are being awoken to the pilot announcing twenty minutes till our arrival in Puerto Morelos. Hmmm, he is free to name our destination now. *Well played Grayson.* He looks down at me while placing feather light strokes to my stomach. "We have time for one last quickie before the plane descends," he says wiggling his eyebrows.

"You're such a sex fiend," I giggle.

"Yes and you love me. I'm your sex fiend."

"Yes you are baby," I nod. I plant a playful kiss to his lips and needless to say he brings us to one more orgasm before we land.

WE ARRIVE AT Dreams Riviera Cancun around four in the afternoon. I welcome the eighty-degree weather. Grayson and I changed into summer wear after our second mile-high encounter. Island music fills the air as we walk up to the entrance. We are greeted with cold scented towels on a tray to wipe our faces and some sort of fruit infused water. The lobby is open to the elements, allowing the airy breeze to add to its exotic elegance. If the lobby is this beautiful, I can wait to see our room. I've never been anywhere, let alone out of the country. I'm so giddy right now. "I love this place Grayson. I may never want to leave," I say clapping my hands. He tucks me under his arm and rubs the top of my head.

"I want to show you the world baby. But we can start with this overnight trip."

chapter
12

I CHECK MY appearance in the mirror once last time. Jordan packed her black strapless Herve Leger bandage dress and Louboutin heels for me to wear. I pair this with the lacy bra and panty set she got me from Agent Provocateur for Christmas. I've been saving this set for something special since I know this set her back a pretty penny. Honestly, I didn't think it would be anytime soon since I had sworn off men. Grayson is in for a treat. I don't attempt to put my hair up since I know he loves it down. Instead, I let it air dry into its natural wavy state. He comes into the bathroom where I am and sees my ensemble for the first time. *Holy hell*. I can see the lust in his eyes as he stalks toward me and slips his hands around my waist.

"I think we need to go right now baby or we're not going to make it." He massages my ass as he says this. He looks quite yummy himself in his linen pants and button down shirt with his sleeves rolled up to his elbows. Even his forearms are sexy.

"I think you're right handsome." He smirks as he slaps my ass. I think that is his favorite thing to do. The sting causes wetness between my legs. "Yeah, like right now," I agree. He chuckles out loud, the perceptive bastard.

"I want that ache you're feeling right now magnified, love. I want you so fucking hot and ready for my cock that your inhibitions take a back seat. Only then will you truly be ready for what's in store for you tonight."

My legs buckle at the hotness of that promise. Dear lord, I'm in trouble. A limo is waiting for us at the front entrance of the hotel. Upon entering, Grayson pours me a glass of vodka cranberry. "No wine tonight?" I ask, inspecting the glass. I'm not really a vodka kind of girl.

"You'll need something a little stronger to start you off baby. I don't want you drunk, but I do want you loose," he winks.

"Loose, eh?"

His smile broadens. "You'll see." I polish off two drinks before he cuts me off. We arrive at what looks to be an abandoned warehouse without any signage indicating this is a place of business.

"Grayson, are you sure this place still exists? There is nothing here. No cars."

"It's an illusion love. Cars are parked in a private garage next door. I told you, only select VIP even knows this place exists." We walk up to the door and Grayson pulls out a key card that he holds in front of a laser looking beam on the side of the door. The lock clicks and we are able to go in. *What the hell?* This place is a dream. You would never guess from the looks of the outside. It is dripping with luxury at every corner. Spiral staircases, neon lights, and glass encased flames have me captured in a visual indulgence.

Some men from the club greet Grayson and they discuss how long it's been since he's been there. He blames his absence on business and introduces me as his girlfriend.

He talks to a man he calls Rick and asks him to set us up in room seven. The man agrees and walks away speaking into his headpiece. "What is room seven?" My nerves show themselves as Grayson leads us over to the bar.

"Two Cokes, please," he says to the waitress. The scantly clad blonde twists her ass a little too hard for my taste, but Grayson pays her no mind.

"Are those Cokes supposed to be the chasers. Where in the hell is the alcohol?" The club looks like any other nightclub, but like Grayson said earlier, it's an illusion. I have a feeling shit is about to get real and I need my liquid courage.

"Just soda while we wait for our room. I want you to walk into this adventure with me with your eyes open. I don't want alcohol to cloud your judgment. No regrets." My knees bounce in anticipation. "No need to be nervous Siobhan. We're following your lead tonight, remember? You control how far we go. Nothing is going to happen that you don't want to happen."

"Okay," I say. That little disclaimer does little to calm my nerves. When he is given the signal, he grabs my hand and we head towards what will forever be engrained in my brain as 'room seven.' The room is dimly lit, but I can see that it is nicely furnished similar to a living room. Grayson uses the remote on the coffee table to start some type slow seductive music.

He takes a seat first and motions for me to take a seat on his lap. I oblige, struggling to find comfort anywhere I can. "Relax baby, it's just you and me." He pushes my hair to one side and begins kissing my neck softly. He finds my lips and I open for him immediately. Our tongues meet in a passionate tango as he deepens this kiss. I feel the beginning of bulge poke me and it makes me wet. The ache is back with a vengeance. I moan into his mouth and he just smiles. His hand slips underneath my dress as though he's tempted to see just how wet I am. "You ready sweetheart?"

"Ready for what?" That's right Grayson. Get me horny first and then pose the question. He points to the curtain, what I originally thought was a window, and tells me that an exhibitionist couple is behind the one-way glass. They can't see us, but they know we're watching. Tonight, we're the voyeurs. Okay so they can't see me. I can do this. I give him a nod and he uses the remote to open the curtains. *Holy shit, this is like watching a live porn movie.* No warm up, just *bam.* They're both completely naked. The room they're in is similar to ours. Grayson pushes another button and their moans and sounds of sex enter the room with us. He eyes me for my reaction and I'm stunned. The guy is hot as hell. Okay not Grayson hot, but damn.

The woman is leggy, petite with boobs as big as mine. I'm slightly jealous that Grayson is seeing her naked. There's a sex swing hanging from the ceiling. The man bends her over the swing, grabs her hair, and plunges into her from behind. This visual has my own sex tingling. I watch as his balls slap against her ass and she bends over further, desperate for him to go deeper. Grayson's hand eases between my legs again and I lock my knees. I'm embarrassed at the wetness he'll find. He nudges my legs apart and smiles devilishly at his findings. He slips one finger inside my panties and I whimper. He works that finger in and out, adding a second and I struggle not to cry out. He pumps me faster and I know what he wants. The woman behind the glass is expressing her ecstasy in ways that I want to right now. I watch as the man palms her breast from behind with one hand and pulls her hair with the other. Shit, I want that. Grayson continues to work me over and I'm nearly there.

"You like the way he's fucking her baby? I know you like it rough."

"Yes," I moan softly.

"They can't see us, but they can hear us love. I'm going to make you fucking scream out my name," he promises as he raises my dress above my waist. I get ready to voice my refusal, but the words die on my tongue when he makes a come hither motion with his fingers.

I squirt every-fucking-where as I scream his name. My leg trembles as he continues his ministrations. I've heard about squirting, hell I've even seen it on the Internet, but I've never experienced it. Fuck me, he has been holding back. That was my most powerful orgasm to date. I look towards the glass and the smile plastered on the couple's face tells me they definitely heard my epic orgasmic pronouncement. "Fuck yeah, that's it love," Grayson says as he steadies my legs. "My dick is so fucking hard right now watching that. You've made quite the mess." And it's true. He had the premonition to raise my dress beforehand, but his pants are soaked.

"I'm sorry," I say looking around for something dry his pants. That's surely going to glow under the neon lights.

"No apologies baby. That was the hottest thing I've ever witnessed. Your face was priceless because you didn't know you could squirt or that I could make you. Shit, I need to fuck you now baby. Please say yes." I nod in the affirmative and he is removing his clothes at lightning speed. I remove the dress and he stops in his tracks. Yes, he has definitely noticed my bra and panty set. The bra is black French lace adorned with Swarovski crystals. The boning is similar to a corset making my girls stand at attention. The thong panties match with a frilled scallop edge. He makes the twirling motion with his finger signaling he wants the entire view so I shamelessly model the set for him.

He rushes me as a guttural groan vibrates from his throat. He picks me up and my legs instantly wraps around his naked frame. He reaches at the front of the bra looking for a clasp and it's not there. He gathers the bra in his fist in frustration and I know that he is planning to rip it. "Grayson, please don't. This bra was a Christmas present." His jaw hardens and I know I better clarify. "Jordan bought me this set because I would never buy something like this for myself." He releases the fabric and puts me down.

"Fine. Strip now love. You have five seconds before that tease you're wearing is shreds." He doesn't have to tell me twice. I'm naked and primed for him in a nanosecond. He picks me up again and I wrap my legs around his chiseled waist. His cock jumps up to greet me and nudges at my entrance. He walks us over to the glass and my heart jumps in my throat. "Remember they can't see us love. This room is for voyeurism, but there is a reason I picked room seven."

"Why is that?" I ask, afraid of the answer.

"Dual purpose sweetheart. This is the only room that can be reversed for an exhibitionist with a push of a button." *Holy, shit. I can't breathe.* "The button is right here on this wall so it's not mistakenly pushed by the remote. Give the word baby and we will become the stars of the show. No pressure. Your choice."

A plethora of emotions flood me, hesitancy, fear, and

doubt are at the forefront. At the same time, I want to experience letting go. I want to be daring, bold, and the vixen this gorgeous man deserves. He chose to open this part of his world to me and show me a side of him that not many know about. I love and trust him completely. And it is at this moment that I know that I'm going to step out on the ledge with him. "Push the button Grayson," I whisper. He quirks a single eyebrow at me and panty melting smile spreads across his face.

"Are you absolutely sure?" he questions, allowing me a chance to recant.

"Yes. Don't let me fall." He stares deep into my eyes with an intensity that sears me to the spot. It is without a doubt, that he understands that I'm speaking metaphorically about this ledge we're sharing and not about him literally dropping me.

"Never," he promises. I was curious on how this transition would occur, how this magical button would suddenly make us visible to the people on the other side of the glass. To my dismay, another layer of glass lowers from the interior side of their room, sparking their attention. After the other glass is lowered, the one on our side begins to ascend and my heart beat quickens. This is it. Without putting me down, he walks over and presses the remote once again. A wall mounted swing drops and my mouth gapes open. I chance a look at the exhibitionist couple and they're busy with their own sexual acts.

Grayson sits me in the swing with one strap under my butt and one at my back for support. He steps back and gives me a devious smile. "I love you like this. So trusting and so ready." He walks away and I follow his movement across the room. He kneels down and retrieves a bottle of white wine from the hidden wine cooler. The wine glasses are to his right on the wet bar. He pours one glass and makes his way back over to me. "Sip on this love." He hands me the glass. As I take the first sip, he takes my legs, one and then the other and slips them through the loops of the swing. The net result is that I'm spread eagle for him. I now take a gulp of my wine, intentionally keeping my eyes in this room. He drops down to his knees and grasps my thighs to bring my pussy eye level with his face. I empty my glass in one chug as my anxiety rears its ugly head again. He begins applying tender kisses to my inner thighs, igniting a path of scorching heat in its wake. I begin to throb, now anxious for a different reason. The ache intensifies as he lingers in the general vicinity where I want his mouth the most.

"Please Grayson," I beg.

"What do you want love?" His eyes dance with mischief as he taunts me. "I want to hear the words."

"I want you to lick me," I say hesitantly, aware that the other couple can hear us. I refuse to look their way for fear that I will lose my bravado.

"That doesn't sound like words of conviction, love. In fact, you sound uncertain." He swipes his tongue in an upward motion once before winking at me. My hips buck, but he pulls away. "Now, tell me again what do you want?"

"I fucking want you to taste me. Make me come. Damn you," I say flustered. I'm horny beyond belief. He chuckles softly.

"That's what I want to hear. You're past shyness baby. Ashton and Claudia over there are waiting to see me devour your sweet little pussy." Oh god, they are watching us. I can't focus on them. Instead, I'm in this moment with him. He licks me again, but this time he doesn't relent. He twirls his talented tongue around my clit and I throw my head back in ecstasy. He sucks and pulls at my nub until my legs are quaking. I toss my now empty wine glass towards the carpeted floor away from us, knowing that it shouldn't break. I grab his hair and grind my pussy against his tongue. This spurs him on more. He sucks and licks me with wild abandonment, lapping up my juices with fervor. I scream his name as my orgasm overtakes me while Grayson continues his assault. He inserts two fingers and begins a pumping motion as he continues to suck on my clit. I can't take any more. Once again he crooks his finger, finding my g-spot and I am squirting. *Holy shit.*

"I'll never get tired of that," he brags. He stands and impales me with one thrust. It feels so good.

chapter
13

WITH EACH THRUST, my breasts bounces in time with his rhythm. Grayson watches them with apt attention as he makes my body sing. He grabs a fist full of my hair and pulls. Not enough to cause me severe pain, but to heighten my pleasure. I crave his brand of dominance. His pounding picks up and in my sexual haze, I allow myself to look over at the couple in the next room. Their eyes are both focused on us as the man drives into her. To my surprise, I hold their gaze as Grayson goes even deeper. I watch as the man's face contorts as the pleasure consumes him. The woman cries out as he works her over. Not to be out done, Grayson cranks up the intensity. He spreads my legs even more, angles his hips and does that slow grind that makes me come undone. My control snaps and I buck against him, desperate for my own release. He leans me toward him, before capturing my lips in a sensual kiss, totally changing the moment we've created. He releases my lips and our eyes meet. His look is covetous as he empties himself in me. As I follow his lead, I know that our relationship is forever changed. "Thank you," he mouths. Neither of us makes a move. We're content to bask in the afterglow of the connection we just made. He slowly removes my legs from the loops and then lifts me from the straps.

When he sets me down, my legs buckle from being spread so long. He catches me by the waist and helps me over to the sofa. It is now that I notice that the other couple has already made their exit. "Sit here and I'm just going to get a towel to clean you up." He disappears into a small room adjoining this one; I'm guessing the bathroom. He comes back and kneels so that he can wipe me down. Shortly after, there are a couple of sharp knocks to our door and I jump. "It's okay love. It's just Rick bringing me some more pants." This man's reach and connections knows no bounds. I shield my body with my dress, but Grayson doesn't let him in. He grabs the jeans from the door and slips them on commando. The vision of him walking towards me shirtless and bare feet in his jeans is a sight people would pay money for. The jeans sit low on his hips, showcasing his fuck me lines. His powerful thighs draw your attention with every step and his ab muscles are etched in perfection. "You see something you like?" He grins.

"Yep," I say simply.

"Get dressed sweetheart. I'm ready to head back to the hotel. I need you in a bed." I'm ready to go too. Tonight has been exhilarating and definitely pushed me past my boundaries, but I don't have any regrets. I love Grayson with every fiber of my being and that means that I accept every facet that makes him who he is.

"ROOM SERVICE," A male voice sounds on the other side of the door, followed by a knock. I look to Grayson's side of the bed, but I'm alone. The sound of the shower echoes behind me so I guess that means I need to get up. I quickly grab the robe from the hook on the wall and open the door. My thigh muscles and intimate parts ache in protest. Grayson really did a number on me last night. I push past the soreness and manage to open the door. The guy walks in pushing a cart with covered domes of food. It all smells so delicious. While he uncovers it all, I make my way to the closet safe to retrieve my purse. Grayson rounds the corner in nothing but a towel wrapped around his waist. *Hot damn.* It appears my lady parts have no clue about self-preservation.

"What are you doing," he says, looking at my hand in my purse.

"I was getting a tip for the food."

"I'll take care of it. Come." His mere mention of come has my mind thinking of the alternative definition of the word. I've become such a horn dog. Nobody has ever made me feel or act this way. I watch as he pulls his wallet from his jean pocket and hands the guy a hundred dollar bill. Uh, yeah. That is so not what I intended to give him so he's lucky that Grayson finished his shower. The guy has the biggest smile on his face as he thanks Grayson for his generosity.

"How are you feeling today?" Grayson asks as he moves our food to the table out on the balcony.

"Sore," I smile. Every movement has me reminiscing about last night.

"I thought so. I'll take care of you baby." He ushers me outside and we take a seat. There is a lot of food to choose from, but I stick with waffles, bacon, and my adventurous side tries the century egg. It is a hard-boiled egg with a black speckled outer layer with a green yolk. You only live once, right? Grayson puts a little of everything on his plate. I don't know how he maintains his incredible physique eating the way he does. I kick my chair back on two legs and enjoy the view with my meal. Our suite has an ocean front view. The breeze coming from the ocean is relaxing. We eat in silence, but I can feel Grayson's intensity. He finishes his food first and announces that he is going to run me a bath.

"You're not joining me?" I pout.

"No love. You're too sore. I couldn't possibly be naked with you in the tub and not want to fuck you," he teases. "You will soak and relax. After that, we'll go lounge in the sun for a few hours on the beach before we have to get you home." During my soak, he surprises me by coming in and sitting at the edge of the tub behind me. He tells me to lie back and begins to massage my scalp before moving on to my shoulders.

"You were amazing last night," he begins. "I love that you extended your trust to join me in my world of debauchery because baby you are my world. I am so thankful for you giving me your heart." I close my eyes and let his profession sink in.

"I love you so much Grayson," I confess.

"Your actions shows me more than you know love, but hearing you say those three little words to me will never get old." He leans down and give me a tender forehead kiss. He then leaves me to my soak to reminisce on our wonderful weekend of discovery. When my water begins to turn cold, I finish with a quick bath so I can go find my man. We spend the rest of the day doing absolutely nothing and I couldn't be more content. We sip on cocktails and talk about trivial things, just enjoying each other's company.

I SIT ON the comfy sofa staring out of our bay window. The afternoon rain and endless clouds bring about a sense of gloom. The nasty weather outside matches my inner turmoil that Grayson has left once again for a business trip. We had to cut our basking in the sun time short to head back so he could leave. We left our moment in the sun for the wetness that awaited us. Thunder claps in the sky, shaking our condo.

"Well don't you look pitiful?" Jordan comes and sits next to me on the sofa. "You still have me, you know."

"I know. I just miss him already. I like spending time with him." I continue to watch the flashes of lightening. I count the seconds until the thunder sounds again in the distance. I used to pass the time this way as kid when I was stuck inside. Counting seconds between lightning and thunder is supposed to tell you how far away the lightning is.

"Yeah, it's called the honeymoon phase and you have it bad." She grabs at her hair and makes a sad face. "I've been replaced because I don't have a wiener. Okay a sausage in Grayson's case," she amends. This causes me to giggle.

"What the hell Jordan? Please tell me you haven't been checking out my man's package?"

"Hey, I wasn't trying to. He's the one that came out in a towel that day with a leave-nothing-to-the-imagination bulge. Just saying," she smiles. "I bet it intimidated the hell out of Liam."

"I'm pretty sure Liam wasn't checking out his junk," I say slapping her shoulder.

"Bullshit. Men compare just like women do. That man looked like a wet dream stepping out of your bathroom. I actually felt bad for Liam for a second. And I do mean a second." We laugh our asses off and just like that I'm pulled out of my funk.

"What do you want to do? I'm bored and I've already completed all of my homework," I say gesturing to the coffee table with my books splayed across it.

"Well, we could catch up on all the America's Next Top Model episodes we have on the DVR."

"Jordan, it's storming outside!"

"So, what does that have to do with the price of tea in China?"

"You're supposed you turn off your electronics during a storm," I warn.

"Says who? Is that another one of your childhood memories? God, you are so weird. Nothing is going to happen. All of our electronics are grounded and may trip a breaker, but that's it." She turns on the television, ignoring what she calls my Siobhanisms. Whatever. It's her TV anyway. See if I care if lightning strikes it.

"What are we eating?" I ask, changing the subject. The smell of tomato sauce wafts in the air.

"Baked ziti." She flips through the recordings until she finds ANTM. "You wanna be on top?" she sings.

"Yeah and I'm the weird one? We are such a pair," I chuckle.

CLASSES PASS IN a blur. Unpack messenger bag, take notes, repack messenger bag, and repeat. I've been on autopilot all day. I saw Liam once, but he is still avoiding me. Grayson and I on the other hand, have been seeing each other every moment we can. It's been a month since we visited the sex club in Mexico. We haven't done anything like that since, but I spend weekends with him when he is not being whisked away out of town for business. Sometimes he visits and stays with me during the week to make up for our missed weekends. Jordan and I ensure that we get our girl time in during margarita Mondays and at impromptu times when both of our men are away. Trevor is currently living in Sacramento, but he drives up nearly every weekend. It's funny how things can change in the course of one semester. On the bright side, I think I finally got rid of my stalker. Maybe he or she moved on to their next victim. Whatever the reason, I'm glad that part of my life is resolved.

Jordan's honk of her horn pulls me out of my musings. We have decided that we would just meet at the car rather than the library now that my boot is off. My mother offered to get me another car, but I told her I was fine. Surely, she could use that money toward something else. I'll revisit that idea after graduation, but for now I'm fine carpooling.

"So I was thinking we could have passion fruit margaritas tonight with fried fish and shrimp," Jordan says as we head to the liquor store.

"That sounds yummy to me," I grin.

"One more thing. Bailey called and she wants to come over," she mentions hesitantly.

It's been a month since Bailey has come around. She has been missing in action since my showdown with Vanessa at Drai's. To say that her friendship with Jordan has been strained is an understatement. According Jordan, she speaks when they pass each other on campus, but that has been the extent of their communication. I don't want to piss on the opportunity for them to make up so I reserve my mixed feelings about Bailey. She was so quick to write me off.

"Well good. Maybe you two can work things out. Her problem with me should have never involved you."

"That's bull and you know it. We are a package deal babe. Either she is going to get over this grudge she has against you for secretly dating her brother or get the hell out of our lives. She is being totally unreasonable, especially after what you divulged about Vanessa's scheming."

"You're right of course. I just don't want you to lose a good friend on my behalf." I'm not that girl. 'I don't like her so you can't like her' is so elementary.

"Nonsense. You're my bestie. Everyone else is secondary. Now, I don't want to hear any more about it," she huffs. "Let's go pick out some different margarita flavors. The passion fruit is a must though." That is one of my favorite qualities about Jordan. She goes from a rant to joking in a split second. She gets what she needs off her chest and then she is done with it.

The minute we walk into the condo, I begin making the margaritas while Jordan batters the fish and shrimp in preparation to fry. The girls are due to arrive in an hour. Grayson texts me and I'm momentarily distracted.

Grayson: What are you doing?

Me: Making margaritas for our famous margarita Monday. Bailey is coming over too.

Grayson: Great, maybe you two will bury the hatchet.

Me: I have no hatchet to…

My phone rings in my hand.

"I rather hear your voice love." We missed seeing each other this past weekend. Apparently, his company has been working overtime trying to acquire some business that will majorly enhance their portfolio.

"She's coming to see Jordan not me."

"I wouldn't be so sure," he hints. "I saw her at my parent's place a few hours ago and she'd mentioned how bad she felt for being so hard on you."

"Wow, really? Well, we'll see. She will have to make the first move."

"I really wanted to see you tonight. Maybe everyone will leave early and I can visit you later," he says. "If not, I can always visit you tomorrow night. That would be a torturous wait though."

"You almost sounds like you miss me as much as I miss you," I tease.

"More so love and I'm not the only one."

"Only one, what?"

"That misses you sweetheart."

"Who else misses me," I chide.

"Not who, what? My cock misses you babe," he says in a matter of fact tone. *Holy hell.*

"Watch it lover. I might start thinking you're only in this for the sex," I caution.

"Well you do have some awesome pussy," he laughs. "Just kidding baby. Not about how great it is though. I'm so in love with you that it fucks me up when I have to be away from you for extended periods of time. I long to smell you or just to hear your voice, hence the reason I aborted our text." I smiling so hard my cheeks hurt. It's nice to hear that I'm not alone with this obsession. Jordan would shake her head at us both if she heard this conversation.

"I love you too baby." I blow him a kiss over the phone and Jordan looks over at me while making the gagging motion with her finger.

"I won't keep you from your girls' night baby. Call me later if you can."

"Okay," I promise before ending our call. Jordan starts in on me with her teasing, but I wave her off.

"Save it sister. I've heard some of your mushy phone calls with Trevor. You guys are just as bad." She chuckles and turns back to finish cooking. I use this time to shower and wash away the day. Memories of Grayson and I are everywhere I look, from my bedroom to this bathroom. I truly wish I could skip out this one time to spend time with him. The temptation is there to do just that, but he seems to think Bailey is planning to apologize to Jordan and I tonight. *Damn, the sacrifices we make.*

chapter
14

I SLIP ON a pair of cheer shorts and a tank before heading into the living room. I can hear the voices on the other side of the door so I know the girls have arrived. When I walk out, it is so quiet, you can hear a pin drop. There is instant silence as the girls wait to see how I'm going to react to Bailey. She walks up to me, but I can't get a read on her. As she gets closer, I can see a dried tear stain tracked within her make up. Her eyes are red and still watery as if the damn may break again. I don't know what to say. I'm actually speechless.

"I'm so sorry Siobhan," she begins. Before I can respond, she catches me in a bear hug. It's a silent plea for me to forgive her. I tense up briefly because I'm caught off guard. "I didn't let you explain. I was so angry and then when I saw how hurt Vanessa was, it just made things worse. I blamed you for everything. Vanessa finally confessed her part in this after you outed her and I felt like such a fool," she sniffs.

"I'm sorry I didn't tell you sooner." I can admit my part in this. I should have trusted her to understand.

"I hate that you thought you couldn't tell me, but we all make mistakes. I understand the hesitancy though. You guys didn't start off in a relationship, but even so, it was taboo."

"Yeah, I guess you could say that. I didn't trust telling anyone except Jordan. I was afraid of what would happen if word got out."

"We would've never said anything," Angie assures and Meghan nods her head in agreement.

"Thank you guys. That means a lot. I promise to do better," I promise.

"Awe," Meghan coos and brings us in for a group hug. "This calls for a toast." We each pick up one of the margaritas and clink them together.

"To lasting friendships," Bailey offers.

"To lasting friendships," we all echo. We crank up the music and dance wildly. The more alcohol that courses through our blood, the more off-beat we get. Bailey gets the brilliant idea that each person has to get up on the coffee table and dance to whatever song is thrown at her. When it is my turn, I'm given Bush's "Machinehead." I'm totally rocking it out when I hear a deep sexy laugh. I would know that laugh anywhere. *What the fuck?* Grayson's here. The girls part like the red sea and there stands my Adonis in jeans and a faded V-neck tee. I freeze, in part from embarrassment and partly from shock. The girls all know about our relationship now, but how did he know it would be a good time to show up?

"Nice dance moves baby," he says lifting me from the table. Like clockwork, my legs wrap around his waist.

"What are you doing here?"

"Bailey called me and told me you guys made up and that the coast was clear if I wanted to come see my girl. I forgot to mention when we talked earlier that I told Bailey how much I missed you."

He turns and finds Bailey among the girls. "Thanks Bailey. You ladies can carry on, but I'm taking this one with me," he winks. He slaps my ass in front of them and I know my skin is beet red.

"Just remember those walls aren't sound proof," Jordan warns. Oh. My. God. I'm going to kill her.

"You ladies may need to close your ears then. I haven't seen this little drunken vixen in a week. I won't be responsible for what you overhear." Throw pillows from the sofa come flying at him. Change that. I'm going to kill him first. I bury my face in his shoulder and he laughs.

"Get a room!" Bailey yells in mock exasperation.

Grayson kicks the door open and turns and faces the girls. "Got one. Thanks." Once he closes the door, I jump down.

"I'm so not going to have sex with you with everyone out there, you freaking exhibitionist." He laughs at my candor.

"I didn't have sex in mind love."

"Good, because we would need to wait till everyone leaves."

"Why is that? Is it because you're a screamer and you always end up screaming for my cock?"

"Jesus, you are so vulgar. I'm not a screamer," I huff.

"I beg to differ sweetheart. You've become so beautifully vocal. I can prove it to you."

"You said you weren't thinking about sex," I recall.

"That's because I'm not. I want to fuck you. That's different from having sex. I want raw, sweaty, and unapologetic fucking."

My sex throbs at the dirtiness spewing from his mouth. He unbuttons his pants and from the wiry hair on display I see that he is commando again. That is so fucking sexy. He has managed to get me wet without touching me and he knows it if that smirk he's wearing is anything to go by. He summons me with the crook of his finger. He pulls me in for a kiss, but I have something else in my mind. I drop to my knees and his eyebrow arches in question. I pull his jeans further down and his dick juts to attention. The wetness at the tip is indicative of his anticipation. I stroke him a few times, using his own wetness to help my hand glide over him like silk. The first touch of my tongue to the head of his cock, his hips thrust forward. I lick him base to tip and watch as his face contorts. He throws his head back as I take him to the back of my throat. Guttural sounds rumble within him as I begin to suck and work him with both hands. His girth stretches my mouth wide, but I continue to alternate licking and sucking. I'm driving him absolutely mad and I feel so powerful.

"Fuck, baby. Stop, I'm going to come." He grabs my hair in an attempt to separate himself from me, but I apply more suction. "Shit that feels so good," he pants.

I can tell he is close. He begins to fuck my mouth, all control just gone. His legs tense as he releases his load down my throat. I'm not surprised by the consistency of it this time. I welcome the saltiness of my prize. I lick my lips and wink my eye at him in complete satisfaction that I was able to do this for him. The hungry look in his eyes warns that his appetite is far from being satiated. He pulls his jeans off in a rush and I know that any thought of waiting until my friends leave to fuck me has just blown up in my face. I've lit the fire and now he's taking the lead. He yanks my top and bra off before throwing me on the bed.

"Your turn baby. Let's see if you can keep from screaming," he challenges. *Game on.* He stealthily climbs on the bed and hovers over me. He eases my shorts down my hips with a devilish grin. Right now I'm his prey and I love it. I have his complete attention. "You're taking a page out of my book and going commando," he slides a finger between my legs and I whimper. "Somehow I don't think you stand a chance love. You're soaking wet already. This pussy is on fire for me." He leans over and grabs something from the pocket of his jeans and he pops the unknown item into his mouth.

I nod, but he doesn't need my affirmation. He throws my legs over his shoulders and buries his face in my sex. The first tentative lick is meant to torment. Its slow, leisurely pace ignites heat in its path. His intent to draw this out is obvious. The tingling sensation that exudes in its wake tells me he is sucking on a mint. "Holy shit," I gasp.

"Hmmm, what's that baby?" He begins to suck on my nub and it is too much. I grasp at the sheet as my body quakes. The sensation intensifies as he plunges his tongue deep. I'm no longer in control of my body or its reaction to this sex god. I vocalize my submission with a scream to rival all others as I'm pushed over the edge in a euphoric haze. "Damn, that was so fucking hot to watch love." His knowing smile speaks volumes. My pussy is still pulsating from the aftermath. I don't care that I just alerted the whole fucking building of my orgasm. I need this man now. I push him flat on his back as I straddle him. "That's it. Take what you need."

"Shut up," I growl and he chuckles. I lower myself onto his hardness and revel in the bliss of him filling me—stretching me wide. Once I'm fully seated, I grind myself on him, going as deep as I can go. I start to slowly bounce up and down, taking control of my pleasure.

The groans from Grayson spur me on. He grabs my hips in a predictable fashion to increase our tempo. His hips thrust upward as he impales me on his cock. "Fuck," he says while bouncing me even faster. It feels like he is going to split me in two, but it hurts so good. He fondles my breasts as they heavily bounce against my chest. Before I know it, I'm being bucked off. He flips us both over and puts me on my hands and knees—doggy style. He enters me from behind and I bite my lip to keep from crying out. He pulls on my hair and I'm done for. The sound of skin slapping against skin echoes across the room as Grayson pounds into me. He leans over me and massages my clit, never losing his rhythm. "Get there babe," he instructs. He doesn't have to tell me twice. I scream into my pillow to muffle the sounds that he has pulled out of me as I come so hard my whole body shakes. Grayson grabs hold of my neck and finds his own release. We both collapse on the bed, totally spent. He pulls me in to cuddle.

"You win," I whisper.

"That love, was an epic fuck. There was no way to keep that one tame and quiet." He gives me his heart-stopping grin and I just melt further into his arms. "My little scream-er. I wouldn't change that ever. I love knowing that I bring out your wild side. I love you." His breath soon evens out and I know that he has fallen asleep. I'm not too far behind him.

THE EARLY MORNING light filters through my blinds, bringing with it a new day. I'm wrapped in muscular arms and there is nowhere else I rather be right now. His masculine scent is my aphrodisiac. He pulls me closer to him, letting me know that he is awake. "Morning baby," he says with a deep rasp sexier than usual.

"Morning." I feel his morning wood pressing against my butt so I back into him.

"Uh-uh, love. I need to be to the office in about thirty minutes. I just wanted to lay here with you for a few more moments. If we start something now, I will definitely be late. I don't think the senior board members will be too happy with me." He gives me a quick peck on the lips and jumps out of the bed to get dressed. "My driver is bringing me a suit to change into during the drive over," he winks.

"So when do I get to see you again?" I pout.

"Well, I may need to head to New York this afternoon to apply some pressure to one of the companies we're pursuing, but I should be back by Friday. The company he runs with his father has been keeping him really busy lately. Luckily his graduate assistant has been able to keep things running. "I'll make it up to you baby." He kisses me once more and then he's gone. I jump in the shower and let the hot water soothe my aches.

When I come out of the room, Jordan is at the counter with some math book open. She is biting her lip in concentration as she works with the formulas. "What are you working on?"

"Some last minute studying for this stupid statistics

class. I put off taking the class until the end, now it's biting me in the ass," she huffs. She slams the book closed. "Well, I'm ready as I'm gonna be so let's go. Sorry I didn't get a chance to make your coffee this morning." I head to the Keurig and pull out two Starbuck's Blonde Veranda Blend. I grab our travel mugs from the dishwasher.

"No worries."

"So, last night," she begins.

"Oh," I groan. "You guys heard us."

"Babe, we heard you. I think that scream made all of our panties wet, with the exception of Bailey who was totally disgusted," she laughs. "Damn, that man must really bring the thunder. I had to call Trevor after that. I had to settle for dirty talk over the phone so I could rub one out," she taunts.

"TMI, Jordan. Geesh!"

"Hey, if you can make us listen to you getting your rocks off, you can listen to me talk about my self-induced orgasm," she chuckles. "We even cranked the music up. We can still hear you guys. The girls left after that." I'm so mortified. I can only imagine the looks I will get the next time I see them. Score one for Grayson. *Kinky bastard.*

I'M SITTING IN my finance class, thankful today is my short day. Maybe I'll head over to the library and conduct some research for my operation's management project. I'm distracted from my planning when the professor walks in and begins preparing for our lecture. I turn on my laptop so that I can take notes, but the buzz of gossip to my right catches my attention when I hear Grayson's name mentioned. Two girls are chatting about a scandal on campus.

"I heard that professor Michaels has been caught dating one of his students. They have evidence to prove that he is sleeping with her," the first girl says. *What the fuck?*

"I've heard that too," the second girl replies. "Amy works part-time in the marketing department and overheard some of the other professors discussing it. Apparently he is currently away on business, but when he gets back, he's in a lot of trouble." *Liam, what the fuck have you done?* I can't breathe. This has to be why he's been avoiding me. I feel like I've been punched in the throat. I have to find him now. I stuff my laptop and supplies back into my messenger bag and rush down the aisle and out the door. The professor glances my way, but begins writing on the board as I leave. I set about a maddening pace as I race toward the practice field. I'm going to kill him. As I approach the gym, Liam is making his way there from the other direction.

chapter
15

"LIAM WAIT," I holler. He looks as though he is hesitant to stop, but he does.

"Siobhan, I don't want to discuss what happened right now. I'm late for practice. I've had a month to think things over and although I'm pissed that you're seeing Professor Michaels, I was wrong for the things I said to you." He has the audacity to look remorseful.

"You're pissed that I'm seeing him so you decide to hurt me more by trying to get him fired. If he goes down, so do I. Can't you see that?"

"What are you talking about?" He stops mid stride and gives me his full attention now.

"Two girls in my class were talking about Grayson sleeping with a student. Apparently it is campus news and he is in a lot of trouble when he gets back into town. What did you do Liam?" He looks genuinely confused. He runs a hand through his already tousled hair.

"Shit Shiv. I'm sorry, but I didn't do this. I haven't been

able to face you because of the names I called you and what I accused you of, but I would never hurt you like this. I don't agree with you seeing him, but I knew there was no way to report him without involving you. You have to believe me. I chose to walk away instead." His eyes belie the truth. Well if it isn't him then who? *That fucking Vanessa.* She has moved forward with the threat she made that day at the hospital.

I have to get in touch with Grayson now. I have to warn him. My fingers tremble as I pull my phone from my purse. "Is there anything I can do Shiv?" I forgot Liam was still standing there.

"Um, no. You go on to practice. Maybe we can talk later. Right now, I have to get to the bottom of this."

"Okay," he says reluctantly. "I'll check on you later." He walks off, but every few steps he turns to look at me. I believe him. Shit, this is so bad. I continue dialing Grayson's number— praying that he is not in a meeting. The call goes through after a few rings.

"Hello," a saucy female voice answers. I know that bitch's voice from anywhere.

"Vanessa, put Grayson on the phone," I demand. I really want to light into her, but I need to make Grayson aware of what's going on first.

"Oh, hello Siobhan," she purrs. Fucking cunt. I know she could see it was me calling from the caller I.D. And what the fuck is she doing with his phone, let alone answering it? "Grayson is busy at the moment with a meeting. Can I take a message?" I want to scream, but I'll be damned if I give this skank the satisfaction.

"Just tell him that I called and that it is very important that he call me back ASAP." God, I just want to tell her I'm on to her shit. She thought that slap was something. I'm going to kick her bony ass.

"I'll be sure to deliver the message," she says. I can hear the underlying sarcasm in her voice. She hangs up before I can say anything else. Damn it. I need Jordan. I dial her number next.

"What's up chic?" she answers her phone on the first ring. I delve into today's events up till now. "Holy shit! Okay where are you now?"

"Outside the football practice field." I'm a nervous wreck and I guess it transcends over the phone.

"Take a deep breath Shiv. Meet me at the car. I'm heading that way now."

"Okay." We end our call and I work to bring my breath back to non-hyperventilating levels. What does this mean for Grayson? Will he lose his job? That will just kill me. Do they even know that I'm that girl? I walk briskly toward the car, hoping Jordan has a solution to this cluster fuck. We meet up at the car and she is immediately giving me a hug.

"It's going to be okay Shiv," she reassures.

"You can't say that for sure Jordan." She is silent for a second because she knows that I'm right. "Do they know the girl is you? Could it be someone else?" I give her my what-the-fuck-look.

"So, you actually think he makes it a common practice to fuck his students?" I snap.

"Of course not. I'm sorry. That was insensitive."

"No, it's okay. I'm just scared. I haven't heard anything yet, but the girls in my class overheard they had evidence."

"I wonder if Grayson's heard anything. I know he is away on business, but surely they've left him a voicemail or something." She gnaws at her lip like she does when she is deep in thought. "We need to call Bailey. Maybe she could give us some clues to Vanessa's state of mind recently."

"Who else could it be Jordan? You should have seen the worried look on Liam's face. I believe him when he says he didn't do this. Now let's consider Vanessa's motives. I slapped her in front of everyone, I told everyone how she was a scheming bitch, Bailey is now friends with us again—against her attempt to alienate us, and worst yet, she feels that I've taken Grayson from her. Ding, ding, ding, we have a winner. The conniving, revengeful, bitch award goes to Vanessa," I say with conviction. "I'm telling you Jordan, you should have heard the smugness in her voice. She purposely didn't answer his phone with professional etiquette. She wanted me to assume the worst, but I'm on to her games."

"She may have been screening his calls to divert the shit storm she cooked up too. I'm with you. I believe she would do anything to sink her hooks into Grayson. She exudes desperation. I should've let you finish her off at the club. Too bad that would have surely ended with you both in jail." Jordan is beyond pissed now. "In hindsight, we could have invited her to one of our margarita Mondays and then let you put the smack down on her ass."

As Jordan pulls away from the school, she calls Bailey and tells her to meet us at our condo. "Should I call and tell my mom so she is not blind-sided with this?" She is going to be so disappointed, especially after the whole Liam fiasco.

"I don't think so. Not yet anyway. There's no need to worry her unnecessarily. Wait and see how much info the school has first and what Grayson's plan is." She's right of course. This is why I needed her. Someone has to be level headed during this shit storm brewing. I'm tempted to call

Grayson's phone again, but only an hour has passed. I just need to know if he's heard anything and that he is okay. This is my worst nightmare realized. When we arrive at our condo, Bailey is already in the parking lot.

"I'm so sorry Shiv. This is not good. We need to come up with a plan, pronto," she suggests. We head upstairs and Jordan brews some chamomile tea. She says it's to help me relax, but I don't know if that's possible.

"Let's brainstorm. What do you know so far?" I share with her the discussion verbatim that the two girls were discussing.

"I think it was Vanessa," Jordan says from the kitchen. Bailey looks doubtful.

"I just can't see her doing that to Grayson," she says looking unsure.

"How else would you explain it? Unless you think it was one of the girls." As soon as this statement is out of my mouth, I want to take it back.

"Of course not," Bailey frowns. "It's just that our suspect pool is shallow. There was no way to out one of you guys without hurting you both. So who would want you both to suffer?" Her nicely threaded eyebrow arches in suspicion.

"Well, I don't think it was Liam." She knows everything that happened that day between Liam and Grayson.

"Are you certain?"

"By that same logic, it can be Vanessa."

"But you can't be certain either way," she pushes.

"I guess not," I admit. I'm pretty sure that Liam didn't do this, but I can't say with absolute certainty. After all, I didn't think he would cheat either.

"Well my vote is still for Vanessa," Jordan chimes in.

"And Liam is not my most favorite person." We sit on the floor around the coffee table sipping on our tea. We're at an impasse. My phone rings and I nearly jump out of my skin. It's Grayson. *Oh, thank god.*

"Oh. My. God. Grayson," I start, but he interrupts me.

"Baby, I know. I just listened to my messages. Please don't worry." His voice is calm, but I'm anything but.

"Are you freaking kidding me? What did the messages say Grayson?"

"I can't really talk now baby. I'm not alone. I left for New York this morning after I left your place, but I'm trying to wrap this up as soon as I can." I can hear the concern in his voice. "Okay I just stepped out of the room for a second. Listen closely love. I need you to take a couple of sick days from class. Have Jordan pick up your assignments if possible."

Shit, it's worse than I thought. "What are you not telling me Grayson?"

"Baby, they have pictures from last semester to prove that we were seeing each other. They want to meet with me when I get back, and they've sent an official letter to the address you have on file. You should be getting it soon. Don't go for the remaining of the week in case they're trying to talk to you first to compare stories. We will figure this out when I get back." Tears threaten to fall, but I hold them back for his sake. True we're in this together, but I don't want him to feel any guiltier than I'm sure he already does. "I'm sorry baby," he says. My heart crumbles and I can't help the sniffle that escapes.

"I'm sorry too."

"Oh baby, please don't cry. Fuck!" he screams out. I can hear male voices on the other end of the line and Grayson assuring them that everything is okay. "I have to get back to my meeting sweetheart, but I'll call you in a couple of hours. Until then, please try to calm down. You won't take the fall for none of this if I have anything to say about it." He blows me a kiss over the phone and then hangs up. Bailey and Jordan stare at me, waiting to get the dish, but I just fall over in a ball and cry.

"Damn, this is not good," Jordan deduces.

She kneels beside me and pushes my hair away from my face as Bailey rubs my back. I'd be lying if she didn't cross my mind as a suspect. What if she did this when we were still feuding and only made up with me to cover her tracks or out of remorse? I'll have to speak to Jordan about it later, but for now, I'll try not to speculate. The girls help me to the sofa and wait for me to calm down enough to share what Grayson told me.

"Damn. I know my brother. He is going to fall on the knife to protect you. We have to find a way to keep you both safe so it won't come to that," Bailey says.

"I wonder what evidence they have. Grayson is right though, you need to hang low until he gets back so the two of you can come up with a plan. My guess is they would want to get your side first since they know he is away. You can't let them corner you," Jordan advises. I listen to the advice from them both, but my heart aches. Life is so fucking unfair. He's not even my professor anymore. It would kill me if I ruin this man's reputation or if I mess up my standing at the school. The collateral damage will be my mother's feelings and the feelings of his family. They were indirectly clear that they didn't want him to be with me anyway. *Holy Shit. What if it was his dad who turned us in?*

Okay so maybe I've become quite the conspiracy theorist, but what if this was a way to kill two birds with one stone? The dad may have wanted to get Grayson to leave me and by losing his job as a professor he would have to focus all his time at their company. I'll have to let Jordan in on that theory as well. I'm pretty sure that accusation wouldn't go over well with Bailey so I'll keep it quiet for now.

"I have a headache so I'm going to lay down now. Maybe the whole sick ruse won't be an act after all," I say begrudgingly. Jordan wipes the tears from her eyes and simply nods. "Thank you for coming over so quickly, Bailey. I appreciate your help."

"Of course," she says waving her hand. "We'll talk more after you've had a chance to talk to Grayson."

"Okay." I agree, but I still have my eye on her. I don't want to discredit our trust again, but the truth is, aside from Jordan, anyone can be a suspect. I continue to my room, close the blinds, and strip down to my panties and bra. I snuggle under my comforter, just barely able to catch a whiff of Grayson's lingering scent. It's enough to bring me some comfort though. I have to believe that we will get through this. Love is not volatile, it's what we make it. This is just one more barrier to get past to find our way to happiness.

MY PHONE RINGS somewhere in my bed and I scramble to find it. By the time I find it in the tangled sheets, it stops ringing. It was Grayson. Three hours has passed. I guess I was both mentally and physically tired. I quickly tap on his name to return his call. He answers on the first ring.

"Hey baby, did I catch you at a bad time?" I look and

see that it is only a few minutes after seven here so that means it's after ten his time.

"No. I took a little nap. That must have been some meeting."

"Sorry. One meeting turned into one giant strategy meeting that continued over dinner." He lets out a deep breath. "I wanted to text you, but I knew that would've had me distracted. Bad enough, I had to know that you were there crying and I wasn't there to comfort you."

"Grayson, I'm fine. I just needed to get that out. All the girly emotional crap will be dealt with and out of the way by the time you get here," I promise.

"You're feelings are not crap and I don't want you to ever hear you say that again. You have the right to be scared and hurt. The good news is that I have one more meeting tomorrow afternoon and then I'm heading straight to you. By this time tomorrow, I should have you in my arms." That's a comforting thought and actually brings the first smile to my face since I overheard the gossip.

chapter
16

JORDAN HAS ALREADY left for class and I find that I need to distract myself from the hell that is my life. Soap making is my go-to form of relaxation so I head to the kitchen and pull out all the ingredients I'm going to need to make Bulgarian lavender soap. I love the fresh scent and soothing qualities of lavender. I connect my phone to the Bluetooth speakers that Jordan keeps in the kitchen. I'm in the mood for some 80's music so I select that playlist. Billy Idol's "Eyes Without a Face" fills the room. I pop some chamomile tea in the Keurig, since I really would be an alcoholic if I grab that glass of wine I really want at eleven in the morning. I put a splash of lavender in my tea and continue on with my soap making. When my batch is complete, I look for something else to keep my mind busy.

I plop in front of the television and scroll through the DVR for some senseless reality show. After coming up empty, I finally decide on Real World on Netflix. The irony is not lost on me. I skip forward to season twenty-one since it looks to be the most interesting. When Jordan comes back from class at two, that's where she finds me half asleep.

"Well somebody had a productive day," she laughs.

"Hey, I made soap," I defend.

"That's what I was speaking of. I can smell the lavender before I opened the door," she laughs harder. "I sure wasn't talking about your Real World vegetation you had going on when I came in."

I can't help but join her in laughter. "Yeah, I kind of needed a distraction," I admit.

"What time is Grayson supposed to get here?" she inquires.

"About seven or eight tonight. Why?" She has that up-to-something look going on.

"You and I are going back to the spa at The Landing for a little rest and relaxation," she smiles

"Jordan…"

"Don't Jordan me. It's done. Go get dressed." I hate to admit it, but a massage may be just what I need. I change quickly into jeans, ankle boots, and a cute top since I know where we're going. I won't get caught looking a hot mess this time. I grab my purse on the way out and we're off. The car ride over to the hotel is filled with various tunes that we sing off key to. I love that Jordan knows just what I need. Once we arrive and change into our robes, she hits me with the idea of getting a Brazilian wax again.

"What the hell is in your infusion water?" I point to the drink the ladies gave us to begin our relaxation. "Miss, miss," I pretend to call out. "I think you put too much crack in hers." Jordan laughs so loud it would be embarrassing if I actually gave a shit. I finish off my drink because let's face it, I need some of what's in her glass.

"Come on. You'll thank me later and I know Grayson will," she winks. That wink is so Grayson and I laugh at the thought.

"Fine." I know that will definitely act as a distraction. Jordan is grinning from ear to ear at her ability to convince me with little persuasion.

"Let's get you buffed and primed for your man. Trevor better hurry up and get his ass out here for a visit or I'm going to replace him," she kids. I know that she is only joking. He just started a new job in Santa Monica so he doesn't have seniority to take many days off yet. She's just missing him.

"That's right. Get me all ready for him and then you'll be complaining about the fuckfest that will be going down in my room," I say for pure shock factor. Mission accomplished. Jordan's mouth is hanging open like a fish. I walk up to her and close her mouth with my finger. "That'll teach you for trying one too many times to hint at our sex life." Score one for me. I don't know how many points she has, but who cares. I'm not counting hers. I laugh to myself.

"Rrrrr, Grayson is making you naughtier. Go Grayson." She gives me the thumbs up and we laugh. These people are going to think that we are so silly. Our masseuses come to get us and take us to separate rooms. I'm given some mist to inhale before I lay face down with my face resting in a hole cut-out. The little Asian lady kneads her knuckles into my back and it feels so heavenly. That is the only thing I remember as slumber takes me under.

Before I know it, the little lady is waking me and telling me that my massage is over. Next stop is the Brazilian wax. This is where it would be nice to have some wine. This lady looks just as sweet as the last one. She smiles and nods at me. She's probably secretly a sadist that is smiling at the pain she is getting ready to inflict on me. And what does that make me you ask? The freaking masochist that is crazy enough to have this done a second time. I dig my nails into my skin and gnaw at my lip like crazy, only to be told that the pain is mental. *Okay lady, whatever you say.*

"See you look pretty, so smooth," she says. My skin looks like an angry shade of pissed off. I thank her and head into the lounge area to find Jordan. She is laying in one of the chaise lounges sipping on another one of those concoctions.

"All done?" Jordan asks

"If you're talking about my wooha, then yes it's done."

"And, we've regressed. You were doing so well with the dirty talk. A work in progress," she chides.

"Oh shut the hell up," I say slapping her shoulder.

"A little better, but I'm going to have to tell Grayson he has his work cut out for him." She has been Mrs. Giggles all afternoon and it's infectious because she has me laughing like a looney tune with her.

ARRIVING BACK AT the condo, we are met by Grayson's limo idling near Jordan's assigned parking spot. Shit, I must have missed his call. I retrieve my phone that I had silenced from my purse and sure enough I have five missed calls from him. His driver lets him out as we park. I run up to him, desperate to offer my apologies.

"I'm so sorry Grayson. We were at the spa and I forgot to turn my ringer back on."

"It's quite okay love. I'm glad you were able to relax."

He mouths a thank you to Jordan and walks us back toward the limo. "I'm taking her home with me," he tells her in way of explanation.

"I don't have any clothes."

"We'll get you new clothes," he offers.

"Don't start. Just let me run up real quick and I'll be back down before you know it," I argue.

"Fine. Please make it quick love." True to my word, I'm back within ten minutes. During my time packing, Jordan told me that she was having the girls over so I don't feel bad about leaving her. When I get back to the limo, Grayson is standing right where I left him. He kisses the top of my head before helping me inside. He hands my overnight bag to Stanley, the driver before scooting in next to me. Silence permeates the car, neither of us wanting to step outside our bubble of love for the shit that is in store for us. Grayson just holds me and I allow myself to be engulfed by his scent.

We arrive at his place and he grabs my hand. That small gesture is enough to settle my heart. God, I love this man. We walk into his kitchen and he seats me at the counter. "Do you want to eat first or talk?" I shake my head.

"I want to stay in our bubble a little longer baby."

"Bubble?" His sexy brow lifts in confusion.

"Yes. The Siobhan and Grayson bubble where it is just us. Bullshit chaos can't penetrate our bubble."

"Hmmm, I see. Can fucking penetrate this bubble?" That's it. I laugh so hard, I swear I'm going to pee myself.

"Yes you perv. Sex is in our bubble."

"I didn't say sex. I was very specific when I said fucking," he teases.

"What is the difference, almighty sexpert?" I'm struggling to maintain my giggles—knowing that he's explained this before.

"Well," he says adopting a proper English accent. "Sex is boring. Fucking is primal, raw, anything goes, messy, gritty, nasty, and the list goes on. Should I continue?" He smirks at me and I want to kiss it off of his freaky face.

"Freak," I accuse.

"You love this freak. Especially when I make you scream the house down."

"I love you even when you're not." He kisses me briefly before slapping my ass.

"Let's get you fed so I can have my way with you," he says. I love that he can put the ugliness of what we're facing aside and just be here with me in this moment. He's giving me time to mentally prepare for the shit storm. Literally, the calm before the storm.

"So a little birdie once told me that your favorite food was Italian—chicken parmesan to be exact," he says as he gathers ingredients from his pantry and fridge.

"Yes, that birdie has a big mouth sometimes, but in this instance, it's okay," I reply in reference to Jordan. I watch as he opens a package of boneless chicken halves while finding a skillet to brown it. We talk nonchalantly about some of our favorite past times and places we would like travel. Paris is at the top of my list. He promises to take me after I graduate and I grin like a Cheshire cat. We sip on some expensive white wine and I swear two glasses has me three sheets to the wind. We eat dinner and then Grayson is carrying me to the bed. He removes my clothes down to my bra and panties. That is the end of my recollection of the night's events.

GRAYSON SITS ON the edge of the bed with a tray in his hand. "Wake up love. You need to eat and we need to talk." I groan before sitting up and he laughs. He runs his hands through his damp hair and I see that he is dressed in business attire. He passes the tray to me and I see that he has made me an omelet, toast, and coffee. I go straight for the coffee so I can fully wake up. I don't get morning people. "It's ten in the morning sweetheart." Oops, I guess I said that out loud.

"So our bubble is over?" I sip on my coffee. I know we need to talk.

"I'm afraid so," he says as he runs his hands through his hair again.

"Sorry sex didn't make its way into our bubble last night."

"Fucking, not sex baby and yeah you were pretty tired. You had a stressful day and needed to rest."

"And tipsy," I remind him.

"That too," he chuckles. "So what do you know already?" His demeanor is serious now.

"Nothing really." I tell him about the gossip I overheard.

"I'm supposed to be meeting with the dean and department heads in an hour so I'll know more then. From the message that was left for me, they have photos of us out together. We didn't really 'go out' together here in the city so I'm not sure how incriminating the photos are. Depending on the photos they have, maybe they can be explained as a mere coincidence, but that is why I didn't want them to have a crack at you first."

"Don't you think it will look suspicious that I suddenly get sick at a time they're looking for me in regarding a potential scandal?" I truly wasn't thinking about this earlier.

"Maybe so, but I rather that, than have them catch you off guard before we know what evidence they have. You have a lot at stake here." He gets up and begins to pace. "I'll find a way to fix this somehow baby. I promise."

"Grayson, what about you? You have a lot at stake here too. I wasn't an innocent bystander in this you know. We both knew the risks." It upsets me that he is harboring this guilt. He didn't act alone.

"I'm more concerned about your future. I may lose my job, but I'm the senior vice president at a company that I'm the heir to. It would kill me, if I have any hand in fucking up your future." He walks over to the window and parts the drapes to let the sunlight in. I can see the anger radiating off him in waves. I get up and walk over to him, hugging him around the waist from behind.

"It would hurt me just as much to know I had a hand in causing you to lose your job, regardless of its necessity to your livelihood. Teaching is your passion and your way of giving back." A tear escapes and the overwhelming fear threatens to suffocate me. He turns and wipes the tear away before pulling me into a hug. He kisses the top of my head and tells me not to worry.

"I will make this right. Please don't worry. My connections run deep baby. I just need to see what evidence they have first and how circumstantial it is." He lifts my face and plants a kiss to my lips. "I need to go in for this meeting, but finish eating and get some rest. I'll be back shortly with more information."

The bedroom door closes behind him and the inkling of bravery I had leaves with him. I push the tray of food aside and cuddle with the sheets that hold his scent. The tears fall harder now until I'm an outright blubbering mess. Why must life be so fickle? Grayson and I have already been through enough crap just to find our way back to each other again. By God, if there is a scale balancing good and bad—life's idiosyncrasies, I'm long overdue for a little good to come my way. I deserve to be happy damn it. I love Grayson and I want us to have a chance to work. This whole situation is just so effed up. Whose business is it that we're seeing each other anyway? I didn't get any special privileges, if anything he was harder on me.

To make things worse, I don't know whom to trust. My main suspicion is Vanessa, but still, I can't discount the others. I can't afford to let my guard down. I wanted to share my suspicion with Grayson this morning or discuss Vanessa answering his phone, but somehow it didn't seem like the appropriate time. He just looked distracted and despondent. He's very intelligent, so I'm sure that he's already deduced some of the same theories that I have. I'll wait to see what he learns in this meeting. Hopefully this will blow over. Not likely, but I can still hope. I consider calling my mother now, but again I decide to hold off just a little longer.

chapter
17

I WAKE TO strong arms snaked around my waist. "Wake up love," Grayson says as he pulls me into him. I turn in his arms and study his face, desperate for any indication that things are going to be okay. Sadness reflects in the depths of cerulean iridescence and I know that any hope of that is lost. He kisses my forehead in the gentle manner he does to inspire comfort, but his attempt is futile. *Just give it to me straight.*

"What did they say?" I ask. My throat and sinuses are clogged from all the crying.

"It's not good. They have pictures of you visiting Hotel Bel-Air as well as the Four Seasons along with more pictures of me coming and going. That could have possibly been explained as a coincidence, but more photos were produced of you getting into my car when we were heading to San Francisco and some recent pictures of you here." *What the fuck?* "Someone has been watching us for a long time baby, gathering evidence. They want to see you by today or they are going to expel you. Apparently, they've sent you an email and regular mail requesting a conference. They weren't fooled by the sudden sickness. I'm so sorry sweetheart." He makes a move to get out of the bed, but I hold on to him.

"Please Grayson. Just hold me," I plead. My world feels unsteady under me and I need him to tell me that we're going to be okay.

He pulls me further into his embrace, but his anguished face belies the remorse that he is feeling. "I'm so sorry I dragged you into this. God damn it," he booms. He rolls onto his back and he runs his hands through his hair. "Just tell them the truth. I came onto to you at the club. I had to have you. I suggested the arrangement." It hurts that he can't see our equality in this.

"Did you tell them about our initial arrangement?"

"No, but I think you should. It will show that I'm a perverted fuck that wanted to use you for sex. Your naivety worked in my favor to use your lust for me against you." He jumps out of the bed now and I can't hold him.

"Is that how you feel?" I ask—voice trembling.

"Yes," he answers simply, but he won't turn and look at me. My heart slams against my chest at his deleterious words. Why is he trying to hurt me? I can't be here right now. I'm about to break. I slide from the bed, but he walks out of the room. Fuck him! I quickly dress in the clothes that I came in yesterday that are folded in a chair in the corner. I don't know where my overnight bag is and I don't care. I'm getting the fuck away from here. So he's hurting, I get that, but I am too. I don't want to call Jordan, but I'll be damned if I let him or his driver take me anywhere.

I don't know the address here, so I'll get it once I step

outside. I can call a cab once I know where the hell I am. I storm out of the room, intent on not looking his way. I don't make it two feet before Grayson is in my path, blocking the door. "Siobhan wait," he pleads.

"Fuck you, you insensitive son of a bitch. You think you're the only one hurting and upset? You think you can bump me back down to the status of your casual fuck? If that's the case, you're fucking delusional," I scream. I'm past irate. The f-bombs are a testament to my fury. Grayson charges me and picks me up like I'm weightless.

"You can't leave me. I'm so sorry. I'm losing my mind because I can't let my indiscretions touch you." He pins me against the wall and buries his head against my neck.

"Well, I'm glad you can sum up our relationship as one big indiscretion. Let me make it easy for you," I hiss.

"No. Shit! I'm not explaining this right. Going into this, I admit… the attraction was purely sexual. I needed to conquer you the same way you wanted to use me as your rebound fuck to get over Liam. I didn't expect and I damn sure wasn't prepared for the feelings that you inspired in me. I never expected to fall in love Siobhan. You have to believe me. You have to know what I said in the room before is not how I currently feel."

He looks up at me and his breath caresses my lips. "I need you to tell them I pursued you baby. I will handle it from there. I've already told them as much, but I need you to confirm my account of how we met and got involved. I will make this go away, but in order to do that, I can't have you trying to save me." I nod in agreement, but I know that won't be the case. He wants me to tell the truth and that is exactly what the dean is going to hear. "Please forgive me. I can't lose you. I'm not upset with you—just myself for not being more cautious for us both. Maybe I shouldn't have gotten involved with you because you were my student, but I'm a selfish bastard."

"If you want me to forgive you, you have to stop with this 'it's all my fault' crap. We both chose to ignore the no fraternization policy for our own self-serving purposes. You didn't act alone. I wanted that arrangement as much as you did, regardless how it originally regressed." He stares into my eyes before bringing his face even closer to mine.

"Okay." That's it. He doesn't argue with me. Instead, he captures my lips in a kiss so tender. It is though he trying to express all of his remaining feelings in this one kiss—the pain, the remorse, and maybe even regret. He says that he is going to fix this and I hope that he actually can.

MY HEART RATE quickens as I climb the steps leading to the office of the dean. Grayson had his driver take me home because he had to head back into the office. Neither one of us thought it would be wise for me to show up to the campus in a limo. I told him that I would borrow Jordan's car instead. She wanted to come with me, but I told her I doubt they would let her come in so I would just see her when I got back. Now as I get closer to the dean's office, I'm scared shitless. I knock on the door, waiting to enter my very definition of hell. Dr. Geer tells me to come in and take a seat. He is straightforward in his approach. He summarizes that I'm being accused of fraternization with a professor during which time I was his student.

"What is your response to this charge Ms. Gallagher?" His stern face has me on edge.

"I admit that I was in a relationship with my professor."

"Was? Do you deny that you are currently still involved?" Shit, Grayson didn't tell me how he answered this. His statement of 'just tell the truth,' comes to the forefront. If I lie, I may contradict what he has already shared and ruin everything. I have no choice, but to be honest as he instructed.

"No. We are still involved." I fidget with the piece of fuzz on my jeans, hoping I'm not digging us in a deeper hole.

"Were you aware of our 'no fraternization policy' at the time you got involved with professor Michaels?"

"Yes sir."

"I need you to expand on that. Explain why you chose to enter a relationship that was against policy and risk your future here at our university?" He might as well have punched me in the gut. His eyes narrow as he leans forward in his seat. Do I share my true frame of mind that had me to act out of character? It may be personally too much to share, but I want him to see that I wasn't some skank just out to bang any professor.

"Honestly?" I begin.

"Is there another alternative? Do you wish to deceive me?" He arches an eyebrow at me in question.

"No sir," I swallow.

"Good. I thought we were off to a good start, honesty wise, so let's keep at it. Continue." I start from my break up Liam and how distraught I was. I explain how I just wanted to feel numb, that I was desperate to make the pain go away. Grayson was attractive and actually caused a spark within me. This momentary distraction helped divert my thoughts away from Liam. I needed more. I was willing to be in a casual relationship with Grayson because I wasn't looking for another committed relationship. Liam had tainted my perception of love's existence. I didn't care that he was my professor. I just craved that feeling he ignited in me that made my break up with Liam hurt a little less.

"Who initiated the 'casual arrangement?'" he asks making air quotes. "Did he approach you?" He eyes me with obvious disgust as he leans back in his chair and begin to rub the stubble on his chin. I can only image what he must think of me, but I must press forward. My knees bounce on their own accord as I continue my recollection of my first run in with Grayson outside of school.

"We had run into each other a couple times because his stepsister, Bailey, is good friends with my best friend. She hosted a pool party at her parents' house and this was my first run in with Gray... I mean professor Michaels, outside of school. I think the attraction was mutual, but we didn't act on it. We went on to see each other again at one of his family gatherings, but it wasn't until we saw each other at Bailey's birthday party that we finally gave in." I feel like I'm over sharing, but I can't stop. I need him to see the picture clearly of how things between Grayson and I evolved. I will not let him think that Grayson was just some pervert professor who coerced me into sleeping with him. I share how he came over that night to apologize for hurting my feelings after pushing me away. He was trying to do the right thing. Grayson explained how hard it was to stay away from me and that ultimately the choice was mine to make. I went to him the next day—sober and willing. Had I not gone to his hotel, there would've never been any escalation or further pursuit on his behalf. Dr. Geer just nods his head at the appropriate times, but I can't get a read on what he's thinking. His brows knit together in disapproval and I feel that I may be making things worse. I gnaw at my bottom lip and dig my nails into my palms as true fear begins to grip me.

"Did he ever share test material with you outside the classroom or other assignments?" His eyes narrow in on me as he watches for any sign of deception.

I was waiting for that accusation to rear its ugly head and there it is. I shake my head vehemently at the absurdness of his question. "Absolutely not! If anything, he was harder on me."

"How so?" he inquires. I tell him about the time that I showed up to class late and how I was reprimanded. He never allowed me to feel as though I was exempt from the rules because of our relationship. I also share that Donovan proctored all of our exams. He asks have I ever been in a relationship with any other professor and I tell him no. Has he been listening? "So what do you think your punishment should be for purposefully breaking the rules? What would you do if you were in my position?" He gets up and walks around his desk and takes a seat on the edge. He is less than two feet from me now and the proximity causes a small bead of sweat to form along my temple. His cold eyes are piercing as he stares down at me—no doubt to intimidate me. How in the fuck am I supposed to answer that question? I don't want to make light of the situation by offering a suggestion that is not comparable to my offense, but I'm sure as hell not going to give him any ideas to make me pay the ultimate price.

"I don't know, sir," I answer begrudgingly. He leans forward even more until he is merely inches from my face. I swallow the lump in my throat. He is toying with me now—

enjoying my discomfort.

"Hmmm," he murmurs. "That answer just tells me that you gave little consideration to the consequences during your quest for…" He pauses for maximum effect. "What did you call it again? Sexual healing?" He stares at me intently and I struggle not to break eye contact. *That is not what I called it, asshole.* I don't dignify his rhetorical question with a reply. Instead I continue to look him in the eye while my knees bounce double time now. He arches a questioning eyebrow before leaning back to the edge of the desk and out of my personal space. He tells me that he only has one last question for me and I almost breathe a sigh of relief. I should have known from the way the statement was posed that this last question would be the ultimate mind fuck.

"Are you willing to walk away from Professor Michaels now if it means the difference between your tenure and expulsion?" *Holy hell.* I've been answering all of his questions as honestly as I can until now. He senses my hesitation and pounces on it. "Let me rephrase the question Ms. Gallagher. Are you willing to throw away your academic standing for Grayson?" Somehow his use of Grayson's name and not as my professor, acts to bring my current situation to present tense— no longer speaking of last semester. Is he really giving me a choice to continue my last remaining months so that I can graduate after his performance of intimidation? His question is a legit one and I can't believe I let love cloud this consideration up to this point.

The answer to his question should be a no brainer, but my heart aches at the thought of being away from Grayson. The responsible choice is clear. I can't throw away all that I've worked for away nor can I disappoint my mother. She has invested and sacrificed so much so that I could get a good education. *Fuck my life. Love is not volatile...life is.*

"I would choose my education," I answer. My lips quiver and tears sting behind my eyes. I just need to hold it together for a little longer. I can't let Dr. Greer see how much that decision would be like ripping my own heart out. He stares at me with uncertainty.

"I appreciate your honesty here today, Ms. Gallagher. There will be an investigation to confirm that you earned the grade that you were given and have no past indiscretions," he says coldly. *There goes that fucking word again.*

"Yes, sir," I quip.

"After reviewing your student records, I did see that you have maintained stellar grades. However, I can't tell you anything at this point. I will meet with the discipline committee after the investigation is complete and we will make a decision at that time on the appropriate course of action."

"Yes sir, I understand." He dismisses me with a wave of his hand and I can't get out of the door fast enough. Although his last question was a reality check, I still don't have a clue how the hell this is all going to play out. I'm just glad to get the hell out that office and away from his scrutiny.

I refuse to lose Grayson and still be kicked out on my ass. My mind is reeling with various scenarios on how this could possibly play out. What is the worst that could happen if the committee decides to punish me? Surely they can't eradicate my entire transcript of classes— maybe just the class I took from Grayson. If they expel me now, I will fail my courses that I'm enrolled in now and that will tank my hard earned GPA. Not to mention, I won't graduate on time. I would have to transfer whatever classes are transferable and spend more money retaking the classes that are not. I'd probably have a black mark against my name. Would another university accept me? I would have to move back home and be away from Grayson. Dr. Greer intentionally made that meeting about my role in this and left Grayson's potential punishment out of the discussion. I know he will have to face his own firing squad... hopefully not literally being fired. Would I lose him in the end anyway? Negative outcomes plague my thoughts. I just need to see him. I won't give him up for anything.

If I'm forced to make that choice, I will just have to endure the few months left until graduation. In the meantime, I will spend all the time with him that I can until a decision is made. I decide to head to Grayson's office. I call Jordan on the drive over to fill her in on the meeting with the dean. Her concern permeates through the phone.

"What if they're watching you? What if how you proceed with Grayson is part of the investigation? What if Dr. Greer was trying to warn you?" All the what-ifs.

"I hope not Jordan because I refuse to lose both Grayson and my academic standing. I will make the right choice if one is actually given to me."

chapter
18

I WALK UP to the building of Michaels' Enterprises. The genius designed architecture looks more like modern art and stretches skyward beyond what the eye can see. I enter the circular revolving doors only to be stopped before reaching the turnstiles. The lobby is massive—it's decor rivaling that of a five star hotel. The receptionist that looks to be in her mid-thirties, motions for me to come over to her desk. Her raven hair is in a slick bun and she is neatly put together in a fitted skirt and blouse. She looks more like an executive than a receptionist. She asks for my name, who I'm here to see, and inquires whether I have an appointment. When I give her Grayson's name, she looks at me skeptically. Here I am in jeans and my hair pulled into a messy bun among all these polished, put together people milling about. She keeps an eye on me as she makes a phone call. She announces my arrival to the person on the other end of the phone and then waits to get approval to send me up. I guess she got the approval she needed because she begins creating me a temporary badge. I guess it would have been smart to notify Grayson that I was on the way. It's nearly five in the afternoon. I didn't even think about the possibility of him having left for the day.

"Okay Ms. Gallagher, you're good to go. Swipe this badge at the turnstile and head up to the corporate offices on the 27th floor. The secretary up there is expecting you."

I thank her for her time and head in the direction that she points to. When I arrive to the 27th floor and walk through the glass doors, an older lady— just as polished, greets me. She informs me that Grayson is finishing a late lunch meeting and should be with me in a minute. She points to his office among what looks like three others on this floor. I take a seat and flip through the pages of the Vogue magazine that was lying on the table in front of me. His door cracks open and Vanessa's laughter fill the air.

"Okay Grayson, I'll see you tonight. Behave," she giggles. My hackles immediately go up. *What in the ever loving fuck?* So here I am hurting over a decision I may have to make and he's here locked behind closed doors with the enemy having lunch and shit. And what the hell does she mean that she'll see him later? Behave? *Ugh.* I should just go. I get up to make my escape, but Vanessa walks out and our eyes meet. She smirks in victory and I want to slap the shit out of her again. I turn to leave instead. I mash the hell out of the elevator buttons.

"Ms. Gallagher," I hear the older secretary call. I refuse to look back. I pound the elevator buttons once more. If Vanessa knows what's good for her, she best not step foot in this elevator with me. She better fucking take the stairs or grab the next one.

The doors finally slide open, but Grayson is too quick.

He grabs me and pushes my back against the wall. His chest is heaving and his stare pierces me to the spot. I can see Vanessa from my peripheral. "Let me go Grayson. Finish your lunch date. Oh I forgot, that's what you have planned for tonight," I hiss.

"God damn it Siobhan. Just stop. Vanessa and I were putting together a presentation for tonight's business dinner with some new clients. We missed lunch so we ordered in so we could continue working."

"So why was she telling you to behave," I challenge.

"Because I was making a joke about how I hope they weren't too stuffy and uptight to enjoy the humor I infused into the presentation." His eyes plead with mine and I know after hearing his explanation I have no right to be mad. It doesn't help that Vanessa is still standing there getting a kick out causing doubt.

"Fine. I'll talk to you later. Have a good meeting." I try to break free and he actually growls.

"Insecurity does not look good on you love," he chastises.

"Fuck you!" I shout. I know part of my frustration is over the whole ordeal with my visit with the dean.

"Gladly sweetheart," he says before slamming his mouth against mine. I didn't see that coming. I push against his chest, but he doesn't budge. His rock hard pecs are firm against my hand. He bites my bottom lip and when I gasp, he pushes his tongue inside. His hand slides down and palms my ass. My traitorous body melts into him. I don't know how he does it, but he brings me into the realm of right now so that the other bullshit temporarily fades into the background.

He deepens the kiss and I can't help the moan that escapes my lips.

"Get a room," Vanessa says in disgust as she pushes the button to call for the elevator.

"Great idea," he says breaking our kiss. He hoists me up so that I'll wrap my legs around his waist. He walks us back toward his office and you can bounce a quarter off Vanessa's face. *Smirk at that bitch.*

"Grayson, what do you think you're doing?"

"You need my attitude adjuster right now babe. It can't wait." Oh dear God. The secretary looks away as we pass by. I'm quite sure she knows what is about to go down. He slaps my ass and I yelp. I know my face is flaming red. "Gloria, you may leave for the day. I'll see you Monday morning to discuss my schedule for the week."

"Certainly sir. You enjoy the rest of your afternoon." I think her face is redder than mine. Of course Grayson is oblivious as he walks us into his office and closes the door.

"You do realize you just embarrassed the hell out of your secretary? She knows that you're planning on having sex in your office."

"I imagine she does know I'm getting ready to 'fuck' my girlfriend in here." His office is two times the size of my bedroom. Contemporary furnishings and state of the art technology adorn the space well. The view overlooking the city is breath taking. I bet it's even more beautiful at night. He sets me down on the leather sofa next to the window before kneeling down to remove my boots.

The adjuster is working and he hasn't even pulled it out yet. I lift my hips so that he can pull my jeans off. "What if someone comes in here?" I ask suddenly thinking about the possibility of someone hearing us.

"It's Friday afternoon love. All of the other executives

on this floor are gone for the day. Gloria was the last to leave. Although, nobody would dare enter without permission anyway," he smiles as he continues to undress me. "We need to work on your trust baby. I don't know what other way to say I just want you." Once he has me completely naked, he lays me back against the sofa and spreads my legs. My feet rest against the coffee table while he enjoys the view. The ceiling to floor windows cast the afternoon light across my body, but I refuse to cover myself. This gorgeous man loves my body and I'm starting to embrace my nudity with him. He begins to undress and I want to lick every sinew of muscle. He strokes himself as he approaches me and the visual has me horny as hell.

"Stand up," he commands. I don't miss the subtle voice change. I love his dominant side. I do as he instructs and he turns me to face the city below. He places my hand on the glass and slightly spreads my feet apart. *Holy hell*. He wants the whole city to watch him fuck me. I don't have long to fret. He enters me from behind and it feels so damn good. "Brace yourself good baby," he warns.

He wraps one hand around my neck and fists my hair with the other. He alternates his grip around my neck while slightly pulling my hair and plunging into me. The varying degrees of roughness have my head spinning and stars dancing behind my eyes. I back my ass into him, loving how deep he's going. "Shit Grayson," I scream out. He picks up the pace and his own guttural groans escape him. He tightens his grip around my neck briefly before releasing and the euphoria that follows is something I've never encountered before. My legs begin to give out from under me as I come the hardest I've ever come in my life. Grayson grabs me by the waist while screaming his own release.

"Fuck, that was epic," Grayson shouts. I'm boneless. What the fuck was that? Epic is an understatement. He carries me over to the sofa and lays us both down with me on his chest. "Just breathe and relax baby. You're feeling the effects of the temporary asphyxiation. He strokes my back and I allow myself to totally relax. I imagine that orgasm I just experienced is what being high feels like. The feeling is indescribable. Grayson is a triple threat. He's gorgeous, smart, rich, dominant, fucks like a stallion, and has sex tricks up his sleeve to completely make you addicted. Okay so maybe he is a sextuple threat. I giggle at my own assessment.

"What's so funny baby?" he asks from underneath me.

"You're a sextuple threat," I chuckle. I look down at him and he just smiles.

"I'm glad you think so baby. And I'm all yours," he says thrusting his hips upward. His erection pokes me and I know my relax time is over. I straddle my knees across his lap and he doesn't need an invitation. He positions himself at my entrance and slides into the hilt. I rock slowly, enjoying how he stretches me. He grabs my ass with both hands and pushes his cock deeper. I watch his face contort in the sexy way it does as I grind against the base of him. He slaps my ass cheek and the sting causes instant wetness. He smiles knowingly. He bounces me harder on his shaft and I begin to whimper his name intelligibly. "That's it. Let go baby. Come for me." He angles his hips in his signature move and I'm falling over the edge. He wraps both of his arms around my waist and his hips piston as he drives into me.

"Fuck!" he comes loudly. I really am spent now. We lay motionless for a few minutes before Grayson gets up gathering his clothes. "I have that dinner in an hour baby. You're welcome to join me," he offers as he pulls open a closet and pull out another suit.

"I don't want to make you late. I would need to go home to shower and change."

"You can shower here with me," he says pointing toward what I'm guessing is the bathroom. "I can have Stanley make a run to one of the department stores not far from here and—"

"Grayson, it's okay. Seriously. Sorry about the melt down earlier. Go to your dinner and come see me after."

"Are you sure?" he asks.

"Absolutely," I reassure.

"Okay, but tonight we need to discuss how your meeting with Dr. Greer went." The change in my demeanor gives me away. "Shit that bad, huh? Damn." I can see him getting worked up.

"He said they still have to investigate. He didn't have any answers for me yet. You just focus on your meeting. We'll talk later." I stand up and push him toward the bathroom.

"Okay. I'll try to make it quick as possible so I can get back to you baby, but for right now, come shower with me." Needless to say we have sex or 'fuck' as he would say, again in the shower causing him to rush around like a mad man afterwards. The drive home allowed me some time to reflect on the day's events and how things may change in the near future. My senior year has been a hell of a year. I've had enough excitement to last a lifetime. If Vanessa is the corporate behind exposing us, what does that mean for us now that she witnessed that we are still together? He might as well have told her he was taking me to his office to bang me for God's sake. What if Jordan's right? What if our continued involvement is part of the investigation? What if Vanessa is feeding them the intel?

JORDAN IS SNUGGLED up with Trevor when I enter the condo. "Look who surprised me with a visit." Her face is going to split open if she grins any harder. We exchange pleasantries and I head to my room. Jordan follows me into my room. "I didn't know he was coming. I'm here if you need me. Do you need to talk?" I don't want to keep her from Trevor. I know how much she misses him and I don't how long he's staying before he has to leave again.

"Jordan, I'm fine. I already told you all that I know so far. Go enjoy your man. We'll talk later."

"Okay. I think he wants to take me to dinner." I can see that she is torn because she thinks she is abandoning me in a time of need.

"Well hurry up and get out then. Grayson is coming over later and we both can't be screaming the walls down. We'll get evicted. How would you explain that to your parents?" I joke. She burst into laughter and I push her out the door. Once the condo is quiet and I'm sure they've left, I head into the kitchen to look through our take out drawer. I decide to keep it simple and order a cheese pizza. While waiting for the delivery I gather the work Jordan brought back from the classes I missed this week. The doorbell rings, but it's too soon for the pizza. Maybe Grayson cut his meeting super short. I'm giddy at the prospect.

I swing the door open wide, ready to greet my man. I freeze at the surprise standing in my doorway. Seems like today is the day for surprise visitors. "Well, are you going to let me in?" Liam asks. I step aside still stunned. I'm not sure how to process the fact that he's here. My paranoia goes in to overdrive. What if he's the one that ratted us out and is here to try to see if I'm still involved with Grayson? It kind of suspicious that after a month of avoiding me he just drops by, without calling might I add.

"What do you want Liam?" My guard is up and I'm sure he can tell.

"I've been worried about you. You dropped that bomb on me the other day and then when I went by a couple of your classes the next day, you weren't there. I was scared that maybe you got expelled." His eyebrows are scrunched in concern, but he is a master at deception.

"No, I haven't been expelled. Not yet anyway. Why didn't you pick up the phone? What if I had company?" Grayson is supposed to come over later and he can't be here.

"What do you mean not yet? Do you think they are going to expel you? Your mom will be so pissed. Have you told her about any of this?"

"No I haven't. I don't know what's going to happen yet so I don't want to worry her unnecessarily.

chapter
19

LIAM SHAKES HIS head to express his disapproval. "I just hope this doesn't end badly for you." That pisses me off. What about Grayson? Is he implying that he wants it to end badly for him? I roll my eyes at his insensitivity.

"You didn't answer my question? Why didn't you call? I could've had company." It's his turn to roll his eyes.

"By company, you mean Professor Michaels?" His disdain for Grayson is apparent.

"Grayson," I correct. "And that is exactly who I mean." The doorbell rings and this time it is the pizza. Liam offers to pay and I shoot him a dirty look. The delivery guy grins at me with a crooked smile.

"How is your night going ma'am?" His attempt at small talk is creepy for some reason.

"Great. Thanks for the quick delivery," I answer lamely. Liam takes the pizza to the kitchen. I hand the guy a twenty-dollar bill and his hand brushes mine a second too long as he takes the money from me. The scorpion tattoo on the back of his hand mocks me. A shiver passes through and rocks me to the core. This guy is either openly flirty or working for a tip. I was going to tip him anyway. I tell him to keep the change and walk toward the door so he can get the hint. After I get rid of the pizza guy, I see that Liam has already grabbed a couple of slices. Some help he is.

"What?" he asks innocently. "You don't mind if I have some pizza do you?"

"Fine time to ask, if I did," I answer with dripping sarcasm. He can be so obtuse.

"Look, I don't want to piss you off. I don't like that you're dating Professor...Grayson," he corrects himself. "I guess what I'm trying to say is that I don't want to lose you as a friend. I didn't call partly because I was scared you wouldn't answer and partly because I knew I needed to tell you this in person. The things I said last time I was here was vile and uncalled for. I wasn't honest with myself on how much I still loved you and when I saw another man, him of all people, walk out of your bathroom, reality came crashing down on me. It broke me. I realized that I had truly lost you and that I only had myself to blame. I stayed away from you this past month as an attempt to heal. For the first time, I experienced just how hurt you must have felt when I cheated." His introspection touches me.

"I know you weren't yourself that day. I knew there was no way you actually thought I was capable of whoring myself out for a grade. I won't lie and deny that it hurt that you could be so harsh." He puts his pizza down and walks around the counter to pull me into a hug.

"I'm so sorry. Please don't hate me. Please tell me I haven't loss our friendship too." I hug him back before pulling away.

"Liam, I can forgive you, but first I have to ask you again. Did you report Grayson?

A lone tear slides down his cheek and it's tearing me up inside to see him hurting. Not from a romantic interest, but as a friend that I have vested time with. "Siobhan, I promise you I didn't report you guys. I'm hurt, but I never want to see you hurt ever again."

"So you understand that in order for us to remain friends, you're going to have accept the man in my life whether that be Grayson or someone else down the road." He nods in understanding. The last residual doubt that he may have been the one to report us disappears. The man standing before me genuinely still loves me and wouldn't do anything to hurt me.

"I don't have to be best friends with the guy, but I respect your choice. Thank you for giving our friendship another shot. I can't even blame Grayson for pummeling my ass. I was out of line."

"Well let's put all that behind us and dig into this pizza," I suggest to lighten the mood. I lose track of time and we're laughing our asses off as we take a walk down memory lane. The doorbell rings a third time and my heart sinks. Shit. I forgot about Grayson.

"I'll get it," Liam offers and I nearly knock him down.

"No. It's Grayson. He's not going to be too happy to see you here." I wipe my suddenly sweaty palms on my jeans and slowly open the door. The murderous look in Grayson's eyes and the jaw twitch hint that he is passed irate.

"What the fuck is this motherfucker doing here?" he booms. "You give me shit about Vanessa having a business lunch in my office and then you have your ex come over a few hours later?" I reach for him, but he moves out of my reach.

"She didn't know I was coming over. I needed to apologize. To you too actually." Liam's last statement surprises me. And from the change in Grayson's posture, I'm guessing he is too. Grayson blows out a deep breath so Liam continues. "I've already apologized to Siobhan for the things I said and the way I behaved. I was out of line. I apologize for the things I said too man. I was just angry and hurt. I respect Siobhan's choices and I wish you two the best. You have a great woman there." Liam heads toward the door, but Grayson's voice stops him. Liam slowly raises his bowed head. His eyebrows knit in curiosity of what Grayson is going to say to him. The pain etched in his features lets me know that speech took everything in him—to fold his cards. Grayson places one hand on his hip and runs his hand through his hair with other. He takes a cleansing breath before walking towards Liam. It's obvious he wasn't expecting his apology.

"I apologize for flying off the handle. My last impression of you wasn't great. I know it took a lot to say what you just did and I can respect that. I love Siobhan fiercely and unconditionally. As long as you are respectful of my presence in her life, I think we'll be fine. Thank you for making amends with her, I know she still cares for you as a friend." The two men in my life shake hands and I couldn't be happier. Jordan will be mad that she missed the reunion. Grayson walks Liam to the door and they even crack a few jokes. A true Kodak moment. After Liam leaves, Grayson walks back over to me.

"I'm sorry I jumped to conclusions," he apologizes again.

"We're even then," I say slyly. "Maybe you need my version of the attitude adjuster."

"Baby, I can promise you if we start something right now, we won't get any talking done and we need to talk," he chides. "Now tell me everything so I can be up to speed." I tell him that I was completely honest. I delve into how the conversation went with Dr. Greer. He flinches from time to time because he doesn't like that I shared the guilt or that I admitted that the final decision to enter into the arrangement was mine, but he told me to tell them everything. He wanted me to tell the truth. He runs his hands through his hair again and grunts. He knows he promised me that he would stop looking at me as the victim in this.

"Dr. Greer said he would meet with the discipline committee after he investigates things further. He wants to make sure that I earned my grade."

"Baby, I told them I was the pursuer just like I said back at my place when you got so upset with me. You just cast the light right back on yourself as having equal guilt in this."

"I did, damn it. How many times do I have to say that? I refuse to let you fall on the sword for me. It would devastate me for you to be persecuted alone for a decision that was ultimately mine to make."

"Baby, I have to go." He makes strides toward the door.

"Why? Are you upset with me now?" I won't run after him.

"No. I just need some time to think. I'm going to have to use a different approach, but I need to move fast. I'll call you," he says as he walks out the door. He doesn't even look back. Okay now I do need Jordan, but I won't interrupt her date. I head to my room and change and slip off my clothes. This was not how I saw the night going. I crawl under my covers with my phone in my hand—willing it to ring. Finally my eyes grow heavy and I let sleep take me to a place less depressing.

IT'S NEARLY NOON and Grayson has yet to call or text me. My will power falters and I pick up my phone to text him.

Me: Are we okay?

Five minutes pass before he answers me.

Grayson: Yes. On the way to Phoenix to officially finalize the deal we closed last night. I'll call you when I get back.

Something is definitely wrong. Why was his text so short and to the point? There was no flirtation—just cold. The dynamics of our relationship shifted last night and I don't know how to fix it. It could be that he is just busy with this new deal, but my gut senses an impending heart break. He is shutting me out by hiding his emotions from me.

I just wish he would tell me again that everything is going to be okay. What is this different approach that he mentioned? I came into the kitchen with the intent to brew some coffee, but now I just sit here at the counter stunned at the lack emotion in Grayson's last text. Trevor walks out of Jordan's room in pajama bottoms and a T-shirt. I didn't even hear them come in last night. I'm pretty sure they made up for lost time, hence the fact that Jordan is sleeping in. She never does that. I just assumed that she didn't bother me because she thought I had Grayson in there. Well at least one of us got some. They're not loud like us.

"Morning," Trevor says as he gather ingredients to make breakfast for Jordan. The scene is endearing. The irony is not lost on me that not too long ago, this was Grayson. I'm glad to see Jordan being doted on, but it also makes me miss my man.

"Morning Trevor," I reply. "Is Jordan still asleep?"

"No she is just laying down now if you want to go talk with her."

"I'll talk with her later." I no longer feel like drinking coffee so I head back to my room.

"Tell Grayson I said hello," Trevor says before I make it to my room. They both think Grayson is here so I don't tell him any better. I don't want Jordan feeling obligated to come check on me.

"Will do," I promise. I crawl back into bed. I think I'll spend the day here. I scroll through my playlist on my phone, searching for tunes to fill the silence. I don't want to be alone with my thoughts. I use Bluetooth to connect to my speakers wirelessly. Natalie Imbruglia's "Torn" fills the room and I sink into the covers as I listen to the lyrics. Two minutes into the song and Jordan is banging on the door. I get up to crack the door open. She tries separately to peep through the door.

"Where is Grayson, Siobhan?"

"Why?"

"I knew it the minute I heard you playing that depressing shit. Move," she says as she pushes her way in. She looks around the room and through the open door to my empty bathroom. "You haven't played a single depressing song since you guys got back together. You forget how well I know you. What the fuck did he do?"

"Nothing Jordan. He's away on business again." I get back in the bed, but she grabs my phone. She pauses the 'depressive music' as she calls it.

"Something is up and you're going to tell me." She sits on the edge of my bed and folds her arms like a petulant child. That makes me laugh.

"Fine, crazy person. I do have some things on my mind, but it isn't anything that can't wait. Your man is making you breakfast after a night of great sex so your ass need to be out there and not in here babysitting me."

She eyes me suspiciously. "You can make jokes all you want, but I can see past your smile Siobhan. Something or someone has you hurting, but I'll give you some time alone. Trevor will be leaving in a couple hours to get on the road before nightfall. I'll be back okay?"

"Yes. Now go before your food gets cold and all his hard work is ruined." I shoo her from my bed and gets up reluctantly. She gets to my doorway and turns with a sheepish grin on her face.

"Did you guys hear us last night?" She still thinks Grayson stayed the night here last night and I don't correct her.

"No. I just know that you never stay in bed that late. I figured you two were playing catch up," I tease. "If you hurry, he can get one in for the road. I won't listen." I turn my music back up and she sticks her tongue out at me. After she leaves, I'm more careful with my music selection. I didn't realize I was that transparent. My playlist is pretty angst filled so I choose the Seal station on Pandora. "Kiss From a Rose" is the first to play. I love this song. I force myself out of bed to do something more productive. I begin cleaning my room and reorganizing the clothes in my closet. My stomach grumbles in protest to my missing break-fast and lunch. I'll just have to hold out until Trevor leaves. I don't want to intrude on their time. For now, the Snickers bar in my purse will have to tide me over.

A few hours pass and I've yet to hear from Grayson. I refuse to call him though. I reached out to him first already. Besides, he said he would call me once got back. I guess I was just hoping that he would change his mind and call me sooner. I distinctly remember him saying that he misses me like crazy when he is away from me from extended periods of time, even though it has only been a day. How could he not want to talk to me, damn it? I'm so deep in thought; I don't hear Jordan until she is standing at the foot of my bed.

"Earth to Shiv," she says, snapping her fingers to get my attention. "What's on your mind?" She sits on my bed—ready to hear the spiel. I tell her everything that has happened up to this point, including Grayson catching Liam here and his subsequent departure after I tell him about my talk with the dean.

"I don't know what to say Shiv. I can see both sides. He wants to protect you from this scandal and you don't want him to take the fall for you. You guys are truly at a stalemate. It shows that he cares or he wouldn't give a shit. It's crappy that he's avoiding you though. Maybe he just needs time like he said—to see how he could protect you both. Just give him time to work things through. Things will work itself out. You'll see." I just hope she's right.

chapter
20

I LET THE water from the shower rain down on me until all that is left is coldness. Jordan sticks her head and hollers from the door. "I made crepes for you so hurry before they get cold."

"I'll be right out." She closes the door and I turn the water off. I slide down the travertine tile and hug my knees. The reality of everything has hit me hard and I feel so out of control. Grayson's disappearing act and silent treatment makes me feel alone and helpless. Jordan is great, but it's not the same. The verdict is still out, yet I feel like I've already lost Grayson. I don't know how much more time passes before my bathroom door cracks open again. I can't bear Jordan seeing me like this so I just keep my head down, until the rustling of clothes peaks my curiosity. Grayson is here and he's taking his clothes off. The shower door opens and I'm frozen in place on the floor. He grabs me by the hand and pulls me up.

"Get up, baby. I'm here now." He wipes my hair away

from my face and forces me to look up at him. The tears I refuse to let fall pick now to make their appearance. Grayson closes his eyes in agony. When he reopens them, he wipes my tears away. "We need to talk sweetheart." I don't like the sadness that colors his voice when he says we need to talk.

"Grayson, you're scaring me." He pinches the bridge of his nose and I can tell he is struggling to choose his words.

"I think we need to take a break."

"What?" I try not yell, but I can't help it. "You avoid me all weekend and then you show up naked in my shower unannounced just to tell me you're breaking up with me?" I can't breathe. I push against him, but he grabs my arms and holds me against him.

"Please listen baby. Calm down. They're going to be watching us. Obviously this is not what I want. I'm not breaking up with you. We just need some time apart to improve our chances for a better outcome."

"What happened to the connections you were talking about? What if our time apart is for nothing? What if they expel me and fire you anyway?" I didn't want to have to make this decision unless it was contingent upon us being cleared.

"I do have connections sweetheart and that is why I'm making this decision now to protect us both. I have ears to the ground on this. Unfortunately, this is not an 'if, then' situation. We need to show that we are willing to adhere to the rules from this point on to get leniency. As it stands, we are still breaking the rules because professors can't date students in any capacity. It doesn't matter that you're no longer my student." His eyes plead with mine to understand.

"How long?" I already miss him and he isn't even gone yet.

"I don't know. If things go the way I plan, you'll be graduating in a few months and none of this will matter." I let my head fall against him. This is what I was afraid of. "We can spend today together though. I'm going to miss you too baby, but it is necessary. Once this is all over I will take you to Paris and we will make up for lost time. I promise." His remembrance of Paris being my dream vacation makes me smile. If I only get today with him, we will have to make the most of it.

"I love you Grayson." I don't say the words to him often, but I need him to hear them in this moment. This is our test. Hopefully this is our final hurdle.

"I love you too baby…with everything that I am." He turns the shower on and grabs my body wash. He pours some on my shower pouf and begins to wash me. I don't have the heart to tell him that I've already showered. He slowly washes my breasts. I watch in lust as his cock begins to harden. I grab it firmly in my now soapy hands and a hiss slips his lips. I stroke him and he hardens even more. He abandons the pouf and picks me up in his signature move, signaling he wants my legs wrapped around his waist. He turns so that my back is against the shower wall.

He enters me slowly, allowing me to savor every inch. This time feels different. We both realize this is our last time before our time apart. His hands grip my ass firmly before sliding to find my rosette. I tighten on instinct. It has been a while since he took me there.

"Relax baby. Push out as I push in and tell me if I hurt you at all." He inserts his index finger a little at a time and I push against his finger as instructed. Once he has his finger in to the knuckle, he pumps his finger in and out of me as he begins impaling me with his cock. I feel so full. The feeling is foreign, but feels so damn good. "That's it love. Let me reclaim this ass so you have something to think about while we're apart. This is mine. You're mine. I need to hear it."

I don't hesitate to shout my answer. "It's yours Grayson. I'm all yours baby!" He pumps me faster from both ends and I'm gluttonous for more. Each thrust upward has me on the propensity of an explosive orgasm. He makes some circling motion with his hips, never stopping from finger fucking my ass and I bite his shoulder. I can't hold on much longer.

"You fucking feel incredible on my cock baby. Let go." He thrusts one more time and I squirt everywhere. *Holy fuck.* I had no idea he could make me gush with his cock too.

The sexy smirk on his face says it all. Just when I think I can't be more impressed with his sexual skills he shows me just how much he's been holding back. His finger slides out of me and grips my thighs with both hands. He pounds me and I feel another impending orgasm. I pull his hair and crash his mouth to mine. He groans his approval and deepens the kiss. His rhythm accelerates as he races toward his own release. I feel his warmness coat me from the inside. Our frenzied kiss slows into more of a slow dance between our tongues. For a second, we pour all of our love for each other into this kiss. He begins palming my breasts and I can feel myself getting wet again around his half-mast cock.

He breaks our kiss to suck on my neck. I angle my head to the side to give him better access. His hands never stop their fondling of my breasts. He rolls my nipples and I whimper. "You have such beautiful tits baby. I want to fuck them." Damn, the filth that he's speaking only causes me to become wetter.

"Okay." I unwrap my legs from around his waist and he lets me down. I drop down to my knees and he arches his eyebrow in question. I grab his cock and I'm rewarded with the wicked lust in his eyes. As I massage and stroke him, his now engorged cock swells to epic proportions.

I lick his slit and a bead of precome coats my tongue. I apply suction just the head and his hips jerk forward. He grabs my hair and begins to fuck my mouth. I open my mouth wider to accommodate his girth. "Shit Siobhan, your mouth is incredible, sweetheart. So fucking hot." I untangle his hands from my hair so that I can take back control. I scrape my teeth along his shaft and he nearly comes undone. "Fuuuuccck!" he shouts. I place his dick between my breasts and he bends just slightly to offset the height difference. I close my breasts around his cock and hold them together with my hands. Grayson takes that as his queue and begins to slide back and forth. As he picks up the pace, I deliver some well-timed licks to the tip of his dick as it protrudes through the top of my breasts. This sets him off into a frenzy. He is titty fucking me and his growls tells me that he is close. I let go of the hold I have on my breasts and quickly take him into my mouth. I take him to the back of my throat as he fists my hair again. His come slides down my throat and I take every drop. When he's done, I lick my lips to make sure I don't miss a drop of my prize. He grins down at me and helps me up.

"My little naughty vixen. I knew you had it in you. That was fucktastic baby!"

"I learned from the best," I tease.

"Oh yeah? And whom would that be love?" His smile broadens and I giggle.

"Are we fishing for a compliment?" He turns the water

back on and begins to wash himself.

"I don't need a compliment love. I think you squirting is the only confirmation I need," he winks. *Cocky bastard.* But he's right. My body tells him everything he needs to know. He washes himself and then washes me before we get out. I'm more than sure my crepes are cold now.

"That was just round one," Grayson grins.

"How many rounds will there be Mr. Sex God?" I ask, dishing it right back.

"Oh, I don't know love, but I do anticipate that a record shattering night is in store for us." My sex clinches at his prediction and his perceptive ass throws his head back in laughter. "Come. Let's get you fed first. Jordan is going to be pissed that I let her crepes get cold."

We dry off and he can't resist smacking my ass while I try to pull up my cheer shorts—commando of course. I'm tempted not to put on a bra under my tank top, but my girls are too big. It only ends up looking obscene. Grayson would love it, but Jordan—not so much. I tried this once before and she told me 'thank you for the peep show' before laughing her ass off. Grayson walks past me, naked, into my room. At first I think he is boycotting clothes for today until I see him reach in to his overnight bag that he has on my bed.

He pulls out a pair of Heather gray sweats and green army tee. I watch as he gets dressed in pure fascination. This shirt hugs his physique like a glove and his bare feet are sexy as hell. "One last eye fuck babe?" He's joking, but the finality of it wipes the lust right off my face. I don't want to think about this being our last night. He recognizes his mistake and reaches for me. "Come on baby. Let's get something to eat. You're going to need your strength. I plan on putting that sexy as body of yours through the paces today," he winks.

Jordan is sitting at the counter with coffee in one hand and flipping through the pages of Elle magazine with the other. When she sees us, she gives me the stink eye. "I knew I should've made lover boy wait out here until you came out. I made you strawberry crepes and you let them get cold," she whines.

"Sorry Jor. Can we pop them in the microwave?" She rolls her eyes in exasperation.

"They won't be the same. You should have saved the sex until after breakfast."

"Who says we were…" She interrupts me.

"I can hear you two. So don't even try lying to me," she warns. Grayson snickers as he puts our crepes and sausage in the microwave. I can't help but laugh too. We are so busted. "Well at least you're in a better mood now," she says sticking her tongue out at me.

"Adjuster," Grayson coughs out intelligibly. Jordan looks at him confused, but I get it. *Smart ass*. After we finish breakfast, I don't think I can move. Jordan had already eaten while everything was still hot so she told me she was off to hang out with the girls at Bailey's place. At least she won't be subject to our last-hurrah-fuckfest. After we eat, I lay on the sofa while Grayson cleans the kitchen. I love that having money doesn't prevent him from being domesticated. He cooks and cleans for me. He's a keeper. I'm trying to stay in the moment and not think about our impending separation, but it's hard. Grayson walks over to me and lifts my head before taking a seat. He places my head back on him and then uses the remote to turn on the television until he finds a recap of last night's basketball game.

"What are you doing mister? Basketball is not part of our fuckfest."

"Fuckfest, huh?" He chuckles at my forwardness and shakes his head. Okay my mouth was running faster than my brain, but we don't have time for me to be shy. I want to devour this man and watching T.V. is not on the agenda. "Tell me what you want love." He is looking down at me, daring me to continue my boldness.

"I want you. I want you to fuck me, possess me, and love me. I want you." He stares at me for a second before getting up.

"Then that is exactly what you're going to get." He clicks the T.V. off and leads me toward the bedroom.

Grayson connects his phone to my Bluetooth speakers and selects a playlist. I watch as he walks over to my chair in the corner. He sits and props his feet up on the ottoman. He crooks his finger, summoning me to him. He pushes play on his phone and Madonna's "Justify My Love" fills the room. His eyes are ravenous as they roam my body.

"Strip," he commands. "Slowly." My tank and shorts are far from sexy, but I will give him all the confidence I can muster. I look him the eyes as I hook my thumbs in my shorts and ease them down. He frees his cock from the confines of his sweat pants and I gasp. Moisture pools between my folds as I watch him stroke himself. I kick my shorts off once they reach my ankles. I go to him and straddle his thighs just so I can have some of that manliness underneath me. I remove my tank and nothing remains, but my bra. He unsnaps the front and watch as my breast fall heavily. My nipples pebble from his attention. He pulls me forward and takes a nipple into his mouth. I lift my hips, ready for him to take me. He doesn't make me wait. He enters me and then captures my lips in a kiss so deep and passionate. He uses his hands to set our pace as he grinds me on his dick.

"Ahh, Grayson."

"That's right love. Feel me. This is me giving myself to you. I belong to you. You own me baby." The slow lovemaking throws me off kilter. I think I just fell a little deeper. We spend the rest of day and night memorizing each other's bodies—alternating between fucking and making love until it's time to say our good-byes.

chapter
21

I ATTEND MY two of my classes and try to keep my head down. The whispers and finger pointing were easy to ignore. It made me aware that the students now knew whom the girl in question was who was sleeping with the professor. No, it's the muffled name calling that really gets to me. The whole student body see me as some skank who whored herself for a good grade. They're not privy to the love that we share. From their perspective our involvement is dirty and wrong. Tears sting behind my eyes, but I refuse to let them fall. I will not let these strangers make me crumble. I quicken my pace to the cafeteria. Maybe I can find a quiet corner to grab lunch before my next class. Behind me, I hear my name being called. I turn and see Jordan running in her stilettos trying to catch up with me. The sight would be funny if I could bring myself to smile.

"Wait up," she calls. When she catches up with me she's panting. "I thought I might find you here. Let's grab some lunch."

"Sure," I say flatly.

"What's up? Why the long face?"

"I'm just not sure if you should be seen with me. I've been labeled the campus whore. You don't want to be guilty by association."

"Shit, you heard the gossip? I'm sorry Shiv, but you know I don't give a rat's ass about these people." As we head to the grill, I tell her how childish people are. Nobody will say shit to my face. They just mumble shit behind my back. *Fucking cowards.*

Jordan tells me to keep my head up and ignore the stupidity. We agree to meet each other at the car after this last class before heading in different directions. I decide to check my mail at the campus post office. It's full since it's been a while since I last checked it, but a letter from the Department of Marketing catches my attention. I open it, only to find that I have another appointment with Dr. Greer this afternoon at 2:30 p.m. My heart rate accelerates and I'm tempted to call Grayson. Did he have to meet with him as well? I pull out my phone to see if I have any missed messages, but there is nothing. Have they wrapped up their investigation? I blow out a deep breath and stuff the mail in my messenger bag. I'm late for class. I guess I'll have my answer in a couple of hours.

I SHOOT JORDAN off a quick text to remind her of the impromptu meeting I have with Dr. Greer before entering his office promptly at 2:30 p.m. He instructs me to have a seat—that they have concluded their investigation. "Originally, our meeting was supposed to include of the other department heads, but due to a recent development, the decision has been made to push forward. The others were going to need to clear their schedules but I told them it was unnecessary," Dr. Greer informs. What does that mean? Does he know about Grayson and I seeing each other this weekend? Am I being expelled? "Ms. Gallagher, after an extensive investigation, it has been determined that you earned your grade." Holy crap, that was quick. Things can't be this simple. I grasp the sides of my chair in anticipation—waiting for the other shoe to drop.

"What does this mean?" I question. I know there's more. What is my punishment?

"It means we are willing to let you finish your time here. You've been an exemplar student to this point. There are some stipulations, however," he cautions. Okay, what's the catch? He arches that damn menacing eyebrow that sets me on edge. His demeanor doesn't scream 'we forgive your behavior,' but at least he's not all in my personal space today. "You can't have any further contact with Professor Michaels for the duration of your time here as a student. Not in any capacity. We are aware of the talk that is already going around campus and we are prepared to make a statement if necessary. Hopefully, with time, this will become old news and the students will move onto another story. I caution you, Ms. Gallagher, if you don't adhere to these simple terms, you will indeed be expelled." His glare pins me to my seat. The words he is not saying are even scarier than the ones spewing from his mouth.

"What's the catch?" I blurt. Grayson and I were already prepared to stay away from each other. Surely they can't allow us to walk away from this without any ramifications. Shit, that's it. What about Grayson? What is going to happen to him?

"There is no catch. I've explained the conditions in which you much comply with in order to remain a student here. We also ask that you don't discuss any details regarding your relationship with the professor or the outcome of this situation. We need this indiscretion to become yesterday's news."

"What about Grayson—I mean Professor Michaels?" I know I should leave well enough alone, but I need to know.

"Ms. Gallagher, I advise you from this point on not to be concerned with affairs of Professor Michaels. He is no longer faculty here and that is all you need to know," he warns.

Holy Shit. That's why I'm getting off so lightly. They're sticking it to Grayson. He gonna take the fall for this. Oh my God. What did he do? I told him that I didn't want this. I try to focus on the warnings that Dr. Greer is issuing, but I can feel the anger building within me.

"That will be all, Ms. Gallagher," he says dismissing me with that demeaning wave off thing he does. I keep my cool long enough to answer him.

"Yes sir," I say simply. I don't even thank him for the opportunity to stay in school because it is at the expense of Grayson. Instead I nod and hurry out the door. I need to find Jordan. I need to use her car again. This is not a conversation that I'm going to have with Grayson over the phone. It's not quite four yet, so he should still be at the office. I call Jordan and she tells me that she got a bite to eat while she waited for me to finish my meeting. We agree to meet at the car. I get there before she does. She finds me pacing in front of the car when she arrives.

"What did you find out?" she asks as she approaches.

Fear resonates in her tone.

"I get to finish school and I still get credit for the class I took with Grayson," I mumble. "Apparently after their 'investigation,' they are satisfied that I did earn my grade." Jordan eyes me closely. She knows that is not the end of it.

She doesn't rejoice for me being in the clear because she knows there is more. "What's the catch Siobhan?"

"They fired Grayson. Dr. Greer said that he is no longer faculty here," I cry. Tears threaten to fall. "I didn't want this. It's not fair Jordan. I ruined his career as a professor. Yes, I know he had a choice too, but that's just it. We were in this together and he took the fall by himself. How can I live with that?" I can no longer hold back the tears.

"I know you're hurting Shiv, but Grayson didn't want this to affect you. I know you don't want to hear this, but he'll be okay. This could have been detrimental to you. How could he have lived with that?" She has a point, but it still bothers me. I have to see him.

"I have to see him Jordan. I need to use your car."

"Shiv, Dr. Greer told you to stay away from him. You don't want to get yourself expelled. Grayson's termination will be in vain," she reasons.

"His self-imposed separation from me will remain intact. I just need to see him. I need answers. What did he do? I can't let him get fired and I just walk away without acknowledging how monumental this is."

"Fine, but be careful. You guys work your shit out and then you get your ass back home. You're going to have to stay away from him after this, until you graduate."

I drop her off at home and head to Grayson's office. The same receptionist is in the lobby. We go through the same routine of her calling to announce my arrival with his secretary before she creates me a temporary badge. When I get to the 27th floor, Gloria escorts me to the conference room and tells me that Grayson will be in shortly. I don't know whether to sit or stand. I walk around the large oval table to stare out the window. The room is eerily quiet except for the drips of coffee brewing from the coffee maker in the corner. The door opens and closes as Grayson enters the room. His eyes are hard.

"What are you doing here Siobhan?" His words are very noticeably hard and abrupt. "Was Dr. Greer not clear that you were to stay away from me?" His abrasiveness is like a gut punch. I go to him, desperate for an inkling of affection.

"He told me you were no longer faculty. Did you get fired? Grayson, what did you do?" I reach to embrace him, but he pushes my hands away. I'm confused because nobody can see us right now.

"I didn't get fired. I walked away and now I'm walking away from you." He turns to leave and I shamelessly grab a hold of his dress shirt.

"What does that mean Grayson?" My voice cracks and my eyes water. Vanessa picks this moment to peek her head in.

"Grayson, our lunch is here," she announces. She looks in my direction with a contemptuous smile. Her eyes convey victory as she casually flips her hair. "Oh hello, Siobhan," she says as an afterthought. I don't bother answering her.

"I'll only be another minute," he assures. My heart breaks just a little more. My hand slips from his shirt. I watch the evil bitch wink at him.

"Okay. I'll have everything set up in my office," she says flirtatiously. Once she leaves, Grayson turns toward me and gives me the final fuck off.

"I told you we needed to take a break and you didn't listen. I can't do this," he hurries out in a hushed tone.

"Do what?" My legs begin to tremble. This can't be happening. Tears flow freely now, but it doesn't deter him. His eyes are cold.

"I can't do *us*. Siobhan. This is me breaking up with you. Don't come here again. You won't be allowed up. Stay away from me." He turns on his heel and begins to walk out.

"Grayson!" I scream. "So you're just going to go back to fucking Vanessa now? Is that it? You told me you loved me." I scoff at my own self internally at how damn cliché I sound, but I can't help it.

Grayson levels a serious stare at me, looking very convincingly unphased actually. "Good bye, Siobhan. See yourself out or security will," he says buttoning up his suit jacket. The mask he has up is glacial and impenetrable. He leaves and I am standing here stunned. Did this really just happen? I will not let myself have a breakdown in the middle of his conference room. Who was that man I just spoke to? How could he be so callus? I'm suffocating on his dismissal. I don't even want to think about him meeting Vanessa for lunch. Will he attempt to fuck me out of his system again? I need to get out of here. I wipe my eyes with the back of my hand and briskly walk out the door.

I don't look at the people milling around the halls or the people in the elevator when I get in. I can feel their eyes on me, but I keep my head down. As I pull out of the parking garage, a light drizzle forms on the windshield. A sense of deja vu' passes over me. Desperate to drown out my own thoughts, I connect my phone to the car speakers and select my 90s playlist. Berlin's "Take My Breath Away" from the movie Top Gun begins playing and I laugh out loud at the irony. I let it play because it is exactly how the fuck I feel. I long to hear those very words. The drive home is on auto-pilot. By the time I walk into our condo, I'm numb. Jordan is sitting there with the girls. They all look up when they see me. I forgot about margarita Monday.

"How did it go?" Jordan asks.

"He broke up with me," I answer flatly. She gets ups and runs to my side.

"Oh Shiv. I'm so sorry babe." I put my hand up. I don't want anyone's pity. I want to maintain this new numbness I've managed to create.

"I'll be in my room. You guys have fun. I'm not in the mood tonight." Meghan and Angie nod in understanding, but Bailey comes over and hugs me.

"I understand. I don't know what happened between you and my brother, but I'll give you space," she says as she pats my back.

Jordan follows me into the room. "Do you want me to get rid of them? We can resume this next week." She watches as I undress and throw my clothes in a pile on the floor along with my messenger bag. I pull my covers back and get into bed.

"No. I'll be fine. I need some time to myself anyway."

"Okay, but only for a couple of hours. I'll wrap it up early tonight and then I'm coming in here so you better just get over it. I'm not leaving you alone." I roll my eyes and she gives me a half smile. Once she leaves I decide to call my mom. I just need to hear her voice. She was actually supposed to come out here this month for a nursing conference, but couldn't get the time off work because a couple of people quit. She is ecstatic to hear from me and wants to talk about my upcoming graduation. I'm glad we don't have to have the alternative conversation. We talk about how things are going at her job and the books she's currently reading. She catches me off guard when she mentions that she would love for us to visit Paris this summer. My numbness shell fucking splinters into a million pieces and the damn breaks.

"Siobhan, what is wrong honey?" I can hear the worry in her voice. I can't tell her the man that possesses my soul promised to take me to Paris after graduation. We were going to finally have a life free of secrecy.

"Nothing Mom," I lie. "Just tears of happiness. I can't believe you remember my love for Paris," I sniffle. Jordan busts through the door, but pauses when she sees me on the phone. Unfortunately, she sees the tears too.

"Of course dear. How could I forget? Your bedroom could've been a tribute to Paris." And she's right. I had everything from posters, figurines, you name it. I even attempted to learn French once, but then gave it up for Spanish since it was more practical in Texas. "Those didn't sound like happy tears Siobhan. Do you have something else you want to talk about?" She's not fooled.

"No. I'll call you back Mom. Jordan just walked in." Jordan yells out a hello.

"Okay. I'll wait to hear from you. Tell Jordan I said hello too. Love you sweetheart."

"Love you too Mom." We hang up and Jordan disappears out of the room. When she comes back I can't help but smile. She has an arm full of popcorn, candy, and miniature bottles of Mondavi cabernet sauvignon. She dumps everything on my bed before rummaging through my nightstand for the T.V. remote. Although I have a T.V.

mounted, I hardly ever watch it in here.

"It hasn't been two hours Jordan—more like thirty minutes," I point out.

"That went out the window when I heard you in here balling your eyes out. The girls understood. Now hush up. This is *Operation Forget Grayson*. Margarita Monday has been revised to movie night." She starts the comedy *21 Jump Street* and I'm laughing my head off within five minutes into the movie. This is exactly what I needed.

chapter
22

THE WEEK PASSES depressingly slow. Each day that I attend class serves as a reminder of the price it costs for me to still be here. The whispers and gossip has increased as people speculate what happened to Professor Michaels. I continue to keep my head down because I don't want to see their accusatory stares. I'll take this as my punishment along with my loss of Grayson. I don't have classes on Fridays, but I'm here to check out a few books from the library. I plan to bury myself in research this weekend for a paper I have due next week. I just need to keep my mind busy. As I finish checking out my books, Lana Del Rey's voice blares from my phone. Damn it, I forgot to silence my phone. I apologize to the librarian for the disturbance as I rush out the door.

"Hey Jor," I answer.

"Hey. Are you on the way back?"

"Yes. You need your car? Sorry it took longer than I thought to find the books I needed." I shift the four books in my hand and quicken my pace to the car.

"No. It's not that. I talked to the girls and we've decided to have a girl's night out at Drai's." The last thing I feel like doing is going out. She must sense my hesitation. "Come on Shiv. Getting out will do you some good. Let your friends be there for you. Then tomorrow you can go back to being a hermit."

I can use the distraction. Although, I don't know how successful that will be since I have memories with Grayson there. Who am I kidding, I have memories with him everywhere so I think the actual distraction will come from the bottom of a bottle. They have plenty of those at Drai's.

"Fine. I'll go under one condition."

"Name it," Jordan replies.

"I don't want this to be a pity party. I don't want the girls to ask me about Grayson or how I'm feeling. I just want this to be like a regular girls' night out."

"Done," she promises. "Now, hurry and get here so we can see what we're going to wear. I'll tell the girls to meet us here."

I'M STANDING IN Jordan's room looking in her full-length mirror. I barely recognize the sexpot reflecting back at me. This bandage dress accentuates every curve and borders on obscene. The keyhole gives an ample peek at my cleavage while the length barely covers my ass. The smokiness of my make up make my gray eyes pop and my red hair falls in endless waves of wildness. I have to admit that I look sexy. I'm not even going to fight Jordan tonight on my appearance. Tonight, I'll allow myself to be someone else other than the depressed person that I've been.

"Damn Shiv. You looking fucking hot. The men are going to go ape shit over you," Angie whistles. Meghan nods in agreement.

"Thank you," Jordan answers on my behalf and Bailey laughs.

We arrive at the club around eleven. We choose to sit in the VIP area on the second floor rather than the cabana area we normally hang out at. As soon as we're seated, Bailey and Jordan order the RMC bottle service that includes Veuve Yellow Label Jeroboam, Belvedere, and Don Julio 1942. We're told that this package comes with a custom light show presentation. I clap my hands in excitement with the girls, but really I'm ready for the tequila. Two hours later and I'm three sheets to the wind. The bass is thumping and the strobe lights flicker. The lights pass over the entrance to the VIP area and I swear my eyes are playing tricks on me until I hear Bailey swear under her breath.

"Shit," she says and the girls follow her eyes. Grayson is here and he is not alone. I instantly recognize the statuesque blonde as Meredith—the woman he brought here for Bailey's birthday. Wow, he didn't waste any time. My heart has just been ripped from my fucking chest. The numbness from the Don Julio has evaporated.

"It's time to go," Jordan says grabbing for her clutch. The pity I didn't want to see is etched in each of their faces.

"Hell no. Fuck him," I hiss. And because I'm a glutton for punishment, I watch as he assists her to take a seat on the sofa a few feet from us. Well at least this time she is not in his lap.

He whispers something in her ear and she fucking giggles. He orders a bottle service for them and she snuggles under him. I feel like I'm going to be sick.

"Jordan is right Shiv. You don't need to sit here and witness my brother here with someone else," Bailey pleads.

"Why not? We aren't together so he's free to do whatever the fuck he wants. And so can I." That gives me an idea. Turnabout is fair play. I immediately start looking around our area until my eyes land on my target down below. I walk right past Grayson and his eyes enlarge when he sees me, but I keep going.

"Wait up," Jordan calls. "Where are you going?"

"I see the guys we met earlier when we first came in. I think I'm ready for that dance now." Mitch, Ayden, and I forget the name of the last guy we hung out the first hour we were here. They moved on when they figured out that we weren't interesting in finding hook ups. Ayden was pretty hot. His muscled physique could almost give Grayson a run for his money. Key word being almost, but he'll be perfect for tonight. Grayson want to fuck me out of his system? Well that can work for me too. It wouldn't be the first time I allowed myself to be under one man to get over another.

"Shiv. I know what you're doing and he will know it too. You don't have to stoop to his level," Jordan says.

"I'm not going to let him ruin my night. Now please go back upstairs. I'll be up there in a bit."

"I hope you know what you're doing," she says before walking away. I saunter up to Ayden and he winks at me.

"Hey gorgeous," he greets. He pulls me into his embrace and I let him. "Can I get you something to drink?" This is just too easy.

"Hmmm, sure," I purr. I extricate my inner sex kitten. "What about your friends?"

"They'll be fine." He walks with me to the bar with his

hand just above my ass. He gets the bartender's attention.

"What will it be? Siobhan right?" he asks. His dimples are mesmerizing.

"Yes. And I'll have three shots of Don Julio."

"You're not fucking around," he laughs. "You heard the lady," he tells the bartender.

"Nope," I say simply. I need to restore that don't-give-a-shit-about-nothing feeling I had earlier. He orders Glend-fiddich 21, neat. He watches in fascination as I knock back all three shots. I excuse myself to go to the ladies room and I'm afraid that he will be gone when I finally get back. The damn line was ridiculous. I've probably been gone for at least twenty minutes. Much to my surprise, he is leaning against the bar sipping on his whiskey when I get back.

"I thought you might have fallen in," he teases. "Come on, let's dance." I feel a little wobbly on my feet now that Don has joined the party, but I let him lead the way.

Calvin Harris's "Blame" blares from the club's speakers and I can feel the alcohol begin to relax me again. I look up to where I know Grayson is seated and I see him actually standing and looking over the rail at me. *What the fuck?* I'll give you something to watch, you hurtful bastard. I pull Ayden into me and begin to grind on him. This guy needs no invitation; he grabs my ass and grinds into me harder. The beat picks up and I'm lost in the music. Ayden's hands are everywhere and I don't care. He begins to suck on my neck and I angle my head to give him better access.

"Damn, you smell so good baby. And this ass is incredible," he says as he give it a squeeze. I can feel my dress inching up, but I can't find it within me to stop him. Before my ass is exposed though, I'm being ripped from his arms. My body slams into pure hardness. When I look up, I'm looking into the coldness of Grayson's eyes. He looks beyond pissed. He has no right. I'm no longer his.

"Let go of me Grayson," I spit, jerking away from him. "I'm going to take Ayden home and fuck you out of my system like you're doing with the twit upstairs." I already forgot her name.

"You heard the lady. Let her go," Ayden says while walking up to Grayson.

"You might want to back the fuck up. Whatever you thought, it's not happening. Can't you see she's drunk or do you not fucking care?" Grayson growls.

"Stop it Grayson. You threw me away and this sexy ass man has no problem picking up your leftovers."

"It's not happening babe. I know you're hurting, but I'm not letting you go through with something you'll regret tomorrow when you're sober." He tightens his grip on me and it pisses me off.

"Fuck you. Go find your date. You have no say over what I do or in this case who I fuck. We're over remember?" I squirm, but he doesn't let me free. "Get the fuck out of here or you will regret it. And that by that, I mean, leave the club," he snarls at Ayden.

"Who do the fuck you think you are asswipe?" Ayden challenges. His other two friends see the altercation and surround Grayson. *Holy Shit.* This is not good. Out of nowhere, four muscled guys in suits surround Ayden's friends. Jordan and the girls are here too as well as his date.

"You really want to do this?" he asks Ayden. "My body-guards are ready and willing to take care of your friends while I smash your fucking face in myself." Grayson cracks his knuckles and Ayden swallows the lump in his throat.

"Fuck you man. I don't have time for this shit. Come

on guys, let's go." Ayden turns and leaves without giving me a second glance. I can't believe Grayson just cock blocked me. And where in the hell did he get bodyguards?

He looks at Jordan. "Take her home now please."

"Fuck you. I'm right here," I spit. I watch as his date grab his hand. The gesture stings and I can't keep the tears from falling.

"Meredith, head on back up and I'll be there in a second," he says. She kisses him on the cheek and walks away. She is so beautiful. "Who is driving you all home tonight?" he asks Bailey.

"We came here in my Range Rover," she confesses. He shakes his head and pinches the bridge of his nose. "Take my driver. Stanley can come back for me and Meredith."

"Fine," she agrees. I'll be damned if I have any part of that limo.

"After you sabotage my hook up you expect me to use your limo to go home knowing that you probably fucked Meredith in that same limo on the way here?" *Unbelievable.* "Fuck you Grayson," I tell him for what seems like the millionth time tonight. It looks like a flash of hurt crosses his face, but I know it can't be. He is the one causing all of this. He broke up with me and he's the one here with another woman. He probably already got his rocks off earlier this week with Vanessa. A leopard never changes its spots. I stomp away from the group—concentrating on not falling in these heels. I rather walk or call a cab. I don't get two feet away from Grayson before he is picking me up and hauling me outside. "I'm not getting in your fucking limo Grayson. I don't want to smell the sex you've been having," I yell.

"Siobhan, please stop. I need you to go home baby. I need to know that you're safe." He takes a deep breath. "I haven't fucked Meredith and I don't plan on it. Please just go and I'll call and talk with you tomorrow when you're sober. My stomach heaves and I know in this moment that Don and Patron are coming back up. Grayson senses it too. I have nowhere to run. The limo is idling in the front of the club. I'm going to hurl in front of everyone. Grayson is quick to act. He grabs the ice bucket from inside the limo and quickly empties the ice on the pavement. He hands it to me and not a moment too soon. I barf into the bucket while he holds my hair. He picks me up and places me in the limo so everyone is not witness to my upchuck fest. He signals for the girls and they pile in the limo with me. When I have nothing left to bring up, he lays me on his lap and wipes my face with a wet towel. He uses one hand to call someone. I'm guessing it is one of his bodyguards because he tells him to see Meredith home. He gives Stanley instructions to pull off. He drops the girls home first before bringing Jordan and I home.

Grayson removes my heels and exits the limo with me in his arms. I lay my head against his chest and try to memorize the smell of him. I must pass out because I have no recollection past this point.

"WAKE UP DRUNKY," Jordan taunts. She pulls the comforter off me and I groan. I reach for the comforter, but this small movement sends an agonizing pain to my head. Last night's events is on replay. I groan again at the ass I made of myself.

"Where is Grayson?" I mumble. My mouth feels like I've been sucking on cotton.

"He left last night. He didn't stay. He tucked you in and then he left." She takes a deep breath. "Shiv, I think Grayson broke up with you for your sake."

"What are you saying Jordan? Are you taking his side? Did you not see the model skank he brought with him to the club last night?" Ow my head hurts.

"Of course not, but you didn't see him last night. I saw the hurt in his eyes at the thought you were going to hook up with someone else. And then when he put you to bed, he kissed your forehead before leaving. He is clearly hurting too. I won't pretend to know all the answers, but there is more to this than he is letting on. I really do think all of this is an illusion to get you to stay away long enough for you to graduate." She could be right. But why go out on dates and at a club that he know that we frequently go to? I need answers. I know I should leave well enough alone, but he's the one that said communication is key this go around. If what Jordan is saying is true, I need to know. We can be adult about this rather than destroying each other to prove a point.

Jordan mentions that Trevor is on the way to pick her up. She doesn't know what he has planned because he says it's a surprise. She rushes off to get ready, but says that we will discuss Grayson later. Pay attention to what his actions are telling you she suggested. His actions are telling me that he is all about having the next woman warm his bed. I manage to pad to my bathroom and take some Tylenol before showering. After I feel somewhat human again, I decide to pay Grayson a visit. I will make him talk to me. I don't want him to take me back, but I do want honest answers. I heard Jordan leave with Trevor a few minutes ago so I can take her car. I have her spare on my key ring. I don't plan on being gone long. I throw on a pair of jeans, T-shirt, and sneakers. I pull my hair in a messy bun. I grab my purse and keys and head out of the door.

I ARRIVE AT Grayson's place in just under thirty minutes. The gates open upon my arrival so I proceed up the drive. My heart plummets when I see Vanessa's red Mercedes SL63 AMG. *So much for him hurting, Jordan.* He's back to fucking Vanessa. I fucking hate him. I get out of the car with the intent on confronting them both. He needs to know that he has been caught in the act. *Fucking bastard.* After today, I will completely write him off. I will finish my three months, graduate, and get the hell out of Los Angeles. My eyes are wide open Jordan and I don't like what I see. When I get up to his door, I still my nerves and prepare myself for this showdown. I lift my hand, but it is pulled behind my back. My other arm is pulled behind me as well. I try to scream, but my mouth is covered by another set of hands. *What the fuck?* Any hope that this is Grayson, dies a sordid death when I catch a glimpse of the man covering my mouth with a rag. He has on a black ski mask. I begin to gag on the vapors releasing from the rag. I struggle to free myself, but weakness begins to overcome me. My stalker has found me. I didn't know there were two of them and now I'm going to die. This is my last lucid thought before blackness overcomes me.

epilogue

Grayson

VANESSA STANDS IN the middle of my living room looking scared shitless of my wrath. She knows I'm not fucking around. I asked her here to talk. The most recent pictures I've recently received are from the time I spent with Siobhan in San Francisco. I needed to question Vanessa in person to check her bullshit meter.

"Grayson, I promise I didn't leak the pictures to the dean. Although I think you can do better than Siobhan, I wouldn't do that to you." She backs up until her back is against the bar. I saunter over to her calculatingly slow until we are mere inches apart. She bows her head, but I lift her chin so that she is forced to look me in the eyes.

"By better, are you talking about yourself Vanessa?" She gasps and murmurs unintelligibly.

"What was that? Fuck it, I'll throw you a bone here so you can save some dignity. You and me will never happen again. What we had was a fuck, but don't confuse that with something it wasn't." Her lips begin to tremble. I fucking hate to see a woman cry. Sad thing is, this is the only way that she will see the reality of our past involvement. I know that she was hoping to have a crack at me when she came over since Siobhan and I are broken up, but she is sadly mistaken. I love Siobhan and I plan to make things right as soon as she graduates, but for now, my ruse is necessary for her benefit.

"Aargh," I growl. "This shouldn't be a surprise to you. I never pretended that we were anything more than friends that occasionally fucked. You were well aware. Or have you forgotten?" She regains her composure and just like that she slips her mask of indifference back up.

"You're right Grayson. You were a nice fuck, but I've had better and I can do better." Her jab at my ego is pointless. "You two deserve each other. I just wonder how in love she'll be with you once she finds out the real truth about Celeste." She smirks as she that jab landed as intended.

"Is that a threat?" My nostrils flare. My past with Celeste is the one thing that can fuck my whole world— jeopardize my future with Siobhan.

"Nope. Not at all Grayson," she smiles victoriously. "I'll be going now." I follow her to the door. I'm ready for her to get the hell out of here. She has managed to take my mind to a place I rather not visit and she knows it.

"Grayson, why is Jordan's Mercedes behind mine?" I follow Vanessa's eyes and sure enough, the car is blocking her in. I run past her toward the car. It has to be Siobhan. God, I can only imagine the thoughts running through her head to see Vanessa here. I know she thinks I've run back to her since this his been our tradition in the past. I get to the car, but it is empty. I look around, but I don't see her. Vanessa leans across her car with her arms folded.

"Siobhan," I yell out. "Where are you baby?" There is no answer. I run into the house to grab my phone. I dial her number, but it only rings before going to voicemail. I call Bailey to get Jordan's number. She tries to find out what is going on, but I tell her I can't talk now.

I dial the first few numbers for Jordan, before Vanessa bursts in the house yelling. "Grayson, I have Siobhan's phone." The current conflict between us is put aside. Although, she can be a bitch, I know that she really does care about me.

"What? Where was it?" I snatch the phone out of her hand and see my missed calls.

"It was in her purse in the car," she says. We exchange worried glances. "How did she even get in the gate without being buzzed in?" That's a great fucking question. How did I not know that she was here? I run to my office to check my security feed. The cameras display black fuzz.

"Fuuucccckk!!!" I yell. I open my desk drawer and pull out the business card I have for Agent Morris from the FBI and hand it to Vanessa. "Call this number on the card and tell them I need agents here now. After that, call my father."

"You don't want to make sure she's not here on the grounds somewhere?" I point to my cameras. Someone cut the feed to the cameras Vanessa. I'm pretty sure they overrode the access to the gate too, allowing themselves, as well as Siobhan, to get in undetected." I fall into my office chair. I can't believe this is happening.

"Do you think this has anything to do with the pictures and the leak to the dean that you were accusing me of." Her eyes are wide. She is genuinely afraid.

"Yes," I say simply. "Please go make these calls for me. I need to see what I can find on these tapes before they cut the feed."

"Anything you need Grayson. We'll find her." She leaves and closes the door behind her.

I slam my hands down on my desk. Fuck, I should have just told her. I started getting warnings of 'I'm on to you' in a manila envelope in my inbox at work. Then came the demands for a million dollars or they would share my dirty secret. The threats were vague in the beginning, but I contacted the FBI anyway and notified them of the attempted extortion. I assumed it was someone who was sour over losing their company to ours during a hostile takeover. My father's start of this company consisted of some illegal practices, but everything's legit now and the past has been buried. I thought whatever this person thought they knew about our company couldn't be proven. A detail was put on me and I continued on as usual. They were pretty much invisible until last night when I got into that altercation with that opportunistic fuck at the club.

When pictures of Siobhan and I were leaked to the dean, I didn't tie the two instances together. My suspicions were between Liam and Vanessa. Hence the reason I broke up with her and started being seen with another woman. I needed to make the break up seem real in case we were being watched. I couldn't share that with her because her rebellious nature wouldn't have gone along with it. I couldn't risk her getting the deal I made with the dean revoked because she refused to stay away from me. It crushed me to see the hurt I caused her. I almost caved last night, but I had to stay strong. And now she's gone. I had a detail put on her as a precaution, but there was no activity reported in relation to her so they backed off.

Now that she is gone, I'll bet anything the two threats are related. She is what they were calling my dirty little secret not my father's old seedy dealings. They are going to use her now to get the millions they couldn't get before. I'm prepared to pay every damn cent. God, I couldn't live with myself if they hurt her. She's my world. I can't go through this shit again. I comb through the video footage, but there's nothing. I put my head on my desk. I feel so fucking helpless. My father walks into my office with Vanessa close behind him.

"The FBI is here son. They're outside now scouring the property, looking for clues to Siobhan's disappearance." I look up at him and I don't attempt to hide my watery eyes. "Stay strong son."

"That's easier said than done. Right now the woman I love is in the custody of some sick fuck who has an ax to grind with me for business that we have done!" I pound the desk again, but I really want to put my fist through a wall.

"You don't know that son. It may be someone we've done business with and it may not. We are a pretty high profile family. Anyone could have seemed you out and realized Siobhan was your weakness." Vanessa sits quietly in the corner listening to it all.

"Your father's right," Agent Morris says walking in. "This was a professional job. Whoever did this, had been studying the habits of you two. They took her quickly and quietly. They are expecting you to crumble so we need you to be strong. If you had a business trip to take, now would be ideal."

"Well I was planning to visit Paris tomorrow to take a look at a potential clothing company I may be interested in.

I'm looking to diversify our portfolio. Maybe Grayson and Vanessa can go in my place," my father speaks up.

"Are you both fucking nuts? The woman I love is missing and you want me to leave the god damn country?" I can't believe this was even suggested. I get up and begin to pace because I'm about to lose it. Vanessa gets up and tries to calm me down, but I shrug away from her.

"Listen for a second Grayson. Siobhan's life may depend on it. Any weakness from you right now can be detrimental. You need to appear as the ruthless business man that can't be broken by pussy." I charge the agent for his insinuation that is merely pussy, but my father grabs me. "You need to show that you are in charge and that the negotiation will be on your terms. They need to feel that they should take what you're offering or they won't get shit. After all, you haven't folded up to this point. If you show weakness, they will up the anty and have you jumping through hoops and giving even more money. In the end, they'll probably kill her anyway. If we do this right and make them work on your terms, it'll give us more time to find her before the close of the deal. You leaving the country will stall their plans because they didn't account for you being gone."

Fuck, I can't believe I'm agreeing to this, but if it is my best chance at saving Siobhan, I'll do it. "When do I leave?" I ask reluctantly.

"Tonight," my father says patting me on the shoulder. Vanessa says she needs to go pack a bag so she was sent with an agent and my driver to collect her things. Agent Garrison and Agent Thompson join Agent Morris and my father to discuss a plan. They want me to be emotionally prepared for when this sick fuck finally calls. After a plan is in place, I pick up the phone to call Jordan. I will leave it to her to inform Siobhan's mother.

"Hello," Jordan answers

"Hey Jordan. This is Grayson."

"Tell Siobhan, I'm going to kick her ass for sneaking off to see you," she teases.

"Jordan, Siobhan has been taken. She's not here." There is silence on the other end of line as she processes what I just said. Her fear is almost palpable as she audibly swallows the lump in her throat.

"Taken where?" she asks shakily.

"She's been kidnapped." My own voice trembles at the reality.

"Noooooooo! Shit Shit Shit," she swears. The line goes silent for a second and I wonder if she's still there. "Grayson, there's something I have to tell you." Trepidation fills me as I wait to hear what has her so distraught with the little information that I've shared thus far.

"Just spill it Jordan," I say impatiently.

"Siobhan has had a stalker since last semester. He or she admitted to tampering with her tire, which caused her accident. I'm so sorry. She convinced me to not to say anything to anyone outside of the officer she confided in because she didn't want people to worry." This is so much fucking worse than I ever could have imagined. *What the fuck?* How could she keep something like this from me? The irony is not lost on me that I kept the fact that someone was black mailing me from her for the same reason. I fall to my knees in the center of my office and my phone falls from my hands. I promise I will kill the sons of bitches responsible for taking her if it's the last thing I do. The agents want strength. Well, there it is. This revenge will fuel me and propel me forward.

forbidden Love playlist

Undisclosed Desires ~ Muse
Win ~ Jarell Perry
Bloodstream ~ Stateless
La La La ~ Naughty Boy
Come As You Are ~ Yuna
All I Want ~ Dawn Golden
Smother ~ Daughter
Lick ~ Joi
Damaged ~ Plumb
Bad Blood ~ Bastille
Eyes Without A Face ~ Billy Idol
Insatiable ~ Prince & The New Power Generation
Love Stoned / I Think She Knows Interlude ~ Justin Timberlake
Numb ~ Linkin Park
Cut ~ Plumb

acknowledgements

First, I would like to thank my readers. This trilogy exists because of you. If you haven't read Forbidden Attraction yet, start there before reading Forbidden Love. Your encouraging words inspire me. Next I want to thank Sarah Hansen, Vanessa Bridges, Stacey Blake, Debra Presley (The Book Enthusiast Promotions), Danese Rexroad, Zenia Guerrero, and Nela Garcia for their critical eyes, encouragement, and incredible talent. They each played a vital role in making Forbidden Love the best it can be. I also want to thank Kassi Bland Cooper and Heather Lane for the awesome teasers, Heather Lane for the amazing book trailer, my kick ass Watson's Wicked Vixen's Pimp Squad (Renee Mckinney, Jacquie Denison, and Kathleen Nichols), my street team-Watson's Wicked Vixens, and Team Grayson. A big thanks goes to all the blogs who participated in reviewing, my cover reveal, blog tour, and release day launch. Last, but certainly not least, I want to thank the woman who has been by my side since August 2014 and has made my writing journey easier – my personal assistant, Renee Mckinney.

about the author

S.R. Watson is a Texas native who resides in Houston with her husband and four children. She is an operating room nurse who has evolved into an author of Erotica and New Adult. She grew up reading the Sweet Valley Series (Twins, High, & University) among others. Back then she would use notebook paper to create stories and cut pictures out of her mother's JC Penney catalogs for the characters she wanted to portray. She ventured away from reading and writing stories when she left home for college to pursue her BSN and then MBA, but picked up reading again in 2012. Her love for the stories written by her favorite indie authors made her decide to pursue own dreams of writing. Her novel Forbidden Attraction (Forbidden Trilogy) is the start of this journey and she looks forward to sharing it with everyone.

When S.R. Watson is not writing, she likes to read, listen to various genres of music, make handmade natural soap, and travel. She is down to earth, loves a nice glass of wine, and is addicted to watching the television series Scandal.

Made in the USA
Charleston, SC
06 March 2015